Secrets Untold

The Lip Gloss Chronicles

Secrets Untold

The Lip Gloss Chronicles

Shelia M. Goss

www.urbanbooks.net

Urban Books, LLC
78 East Industry Court
Deer Park, NY 11729

ISBN 13: 978-1-60162-312-6
ISBN 10: 1-60162-312-7

First Trade Paperback Printing August 2011
Printed in the United States of America

10 9 8 7 6 5 4 3 2 1

*This is a work of fiction. Any references or similarities to ac-
tual events, real people, living, or dead, or to real locales are
intended to give the novel a sense of reality. Any similarity
in other names, characters, places, and incidents is entirely
coincidental.*

Distributed by Kensington Publishing Corp.
Submit Wholesale Orders to:
Kensington Publishing Corp.
C/O Penguin Group (USA) Inc.
Attention: Order Processing
405 Murray Hill Parkway
East Rutherford, NJ 07073-2316
Phone: 1-800-526-0275
Fax: 1-800-227-9604

Secrets Untold

The Lip Gloss Chronicles

Shelia M. Goss

Dedication

This book is dedicated to my two little cousins, Jasmine Hogan and Ellen Jones, and all the fans of The Lip Gloss Chronicles. *Thanks for your e-mails and your comments. Because of you,* Secrets Untold *has been told.*

ACKNOWLEDGMENTS

Before I go any further, I have to acknowledge our Heavenly Father for bestowing on me a gift but most importantly for His grace and mercy.

To my mother who taught me the importance of family. To some special fans: Ari, Charnelle, Asia, Kaytlynn, Macon, Neoshia, Amber, Jayla, Nicole, Nadiya, Kimberly Hagins, Urban Teens Read Group on Facebook, and The Future Leader Readers Book Club in Dallas, Texas. I know I'm forgetting some people, so if you don't see your name here, I'll get you on the next round.

Once again, I have to thank the parents, the librarians, the teachers, the book clubs, The Brown Bookshelf and the reviewers like Urban Reviewers, Urban Teen Reads, APOOO Book Club, RAWSISTAZ, TeensReadToo.com, etc. for spreading the word about *The Lip Gloss Chronicles* (books about sassy teenagers with a lot of heart).

Of course, I can't do an acknowledgment without saying thank you to the people who are responsible for making this book possible: Carl Weber and the rest of the Urban Books staff, such as Natalie Weber, and my agent Dr. Maxine Thompson.

I would also like to thank my fellow authors who write in the YA genre that inspire me: Celeste O. Norfleet, Paula Chase, Ni-Ni Simone, Nikki Carter, Kelli London, ReShonda Tate Billingsley, Carla J. Curtis, and Earl Sewell.

Last, but not least, this book is dedicated to every teenager out there who has a dream. Think it. Believe it and know that you can achieve it. Stay in school and be the best you can be. There's someone out here cheering for you.

Shelia M. Goss

"*I'm a diva*," I sang along with an old Beyoncé song. I snatched my iPod's earpiece out of my left ear as soon as I saw my American history teacher, Mr. Trudeau, walk through the classroom door.

"Ms. Porsha Swint, the next time I catch you with the iPod in class, I will confiscate it," Mr. Trudeau said, as he placed his briefcase on top of his desk.

Busted. "I'm sorry." I looked down as I heard several of my classmates snicker.

Mr. Trudeau removed a stack of stapled sheets of paper from his briefcase. "Clear your desks. Let's see how much you've learned."

I looked at my other classmates and their faces mirrored mine—dread. I hated pop quizzes.

Thirty minutes later, we were grading each other's papers. When I got handed my paper, I frowned when I saw the red mark on the front page. Relief swept through my body when I turned to the second sheet and didn't see any more red marks. I missed one question, which allowed me to remain in my "A" percentile.

At lunch time, I met Danielle Davis and Tara Chance, my two BFFs (best friends forever) at our unofficial designated table in the corner of the cafeteria. Ever since we became juniors at Plano High School, we no longer shared the same classes. We usually ate lunch together because it was the only time we could get together during the school day.

"There's Ken," Tara said, in between bites.

I looked in his direction. The green-eyed monster reared its ugly head at the sight of Ken all up in some other girl's face. I didn't like being jealous. Ken made our stoic school uniforms look like designer wear, because he could have easily been a Calvin Klein model. With looks and brains, Ken in my opinion, had it going on.

Ever since I broke up with my ex-boyfriend Anthony for cheating during Christmas break, boys had been slipping me their numbers, but Kenneth, or Ken for short, was the one who had captured my attention. He was the star of the debate team and had scholarship offers to all the prestigious colleges in state as well as in other parts of the country.

This was the same Ken I watched all up in some other girl's face.

"She needs to get off my man," I said. I was pissed because his actions were disrespectful. Maybe if it didn't happen in front of my two BFFs, I could overlook it, but now I couldn't.

Danielle tapped my arm. "Get ready. Here he comes."

I used my napkin to wipe the food from around my mouth.

Tara said, "You look fine. Now smile."

Seconds later, Ken stood in front of our table. "Hi, ladies," he said, not once taking his eyes off me. "Porsha, what's up?"

"I'm busy," I stated.

"Can we talk after you finish eating?"

The allure of his cologne was bound to break down my defenses. I responded, "I have a test next hour so I don't have time to talk."

"Call me later," he said.

"Ken, look, there's no need for me to play games. I saw you over there huddled up with some girl. Don't think you can come in my face now."

"Aww, that was Lisa. She's like a little sister to me," he replied, not once looking me in the eye.

"Didn't look like no sister to me," Danielle said, right before she picked up her bottle of juice and started drinking it.

"Me neither." By now, I was sitting with my arms crossed.

"I wanted to ask you to the Valentine's dance, but maybe it was a bad idea, since I'm getting all of this attitude," he said.

"I would rather go by myself than go with you," I lied.

"Fine. I'll just go ask Lisa. She'll be glad to go," he replied curtly, before walking away from our table.

I picked up my glass of juice to throw at him, but Tara held my hand, stopping me.

"He's not worth you getting suspended."

"Can you believe it? I actually liked him."

"Jerk," Danielle said.

Tara tried to make light of the situation. "You can always help me babysit the night of the dance."

I rolled my eyes at her. "I don't think so. Danielle, looks like we'll both be going solo."

I spent the rest of the day thinking of a million and one ways to get Ken back. I had the perfect payback. I smiled. Too bad I wouldn't be able to act on it. Texas didn't play when it came to murder, and being fifteen wouldn't stop them from giving me life.

I moved Ken to the back of my mind because the dance was next week and I needed a dress—

something red and hot; something to make Ken and any other boy wish he had chosen me as their date, instead of the one they were with. I couldn't wait for the final bell to ring. Now all I had to do was convince my mom to make a special trip to the Galleria.

My mom drove up in her black Mercedes. She pulled up near us and rolled her window down. "Hi, girls."

"Hi, Ms. Angie," Tara responded.

Angie, was short for Angela. My mom insisted my friends use Ms. Angie instead of Mrs. Swint. My mom said calling her Mrs. Swint made her sound as old as my grandmother. My mom did her best to stay looking young. Most of the time, people mistook us for sisters instead of mother and daughter.

My mom waved. "How's your mom?" she asked.

"Fine," Tara responded.

"Tell her I'll be calling her soon for a girls' night out."

"Girl, I'll call you later," I said as I opened the door and threw my backpack on the backseat. After putting on my seatbelt, I asked, "Can we stop by the Galleria so I can pick out a dress for the Valentine's dance next week?"

"Don't you have something to wear in your closet?"

"No, ma'am," I lied.

"You should. I bought you a red dress for some occasion. You've worn it, what, once."

"But, Mom, you know I can't be seen in the same thing twice." I batted my eyes, flittering my long black eyelashes, hoping my mom could see the desperation.

"Who's your date?" she asked.

"Nobody's asked me out, so I'm going by myself. Well, with Danielle, but by myself." I said a quick prayer, hoping my mom would get me a new dress.

I pouted as we passed the street that would have taken us straight to the Galleria. The only sound in the car was the music my mom had blasting from her car stereo. We were headed to Northwest Highway, which meant only one thing. No. I couldn't get my hopes up. I didn't want another disappointment. A smile swept across my face as my mom steered the car into the North Park Mall parking lot. It wasn't the Galleria, but it would do. I knew exactly what store we could hit for my semi-formal dress.

"We only have an hour because I need to pick up the boys from band practice," my mom stated.

"Thanks, Mom. You always come through," I replied gleefully as I set out on a mission for the perfect dress.

The days leading up to the Valentine's dance seemed to drag on. February the fourteenth marked not only Valentine's Day, but it was the countdown to my sixteenth birthday—a month away. The day for the dance had finally arrived. As I dressed, I talked to Tara.

"Tara, I sure wish you were going." My voice echoed due to me using the speakerphone. I did my best not to mess up my freshly done hair as I pulled the dress over my head.

"You and Dani are so lucky. My mom's just trying to punish me because my dad left."

"When was the last time you saw your dad?" I asked.

"Two months ago. He wants to see us, but she won't let us see him," Tara responded.

"That's messed up. If it were my dad, I would want to see him at least every week."

"It's not like he's not paying child support. He pays and she still trips."

Tara went on and on about her mom and dad and their drama. I halfway listened as I finished getting dressed in front of the mirror. The red knee-length dress was hot. Ken and every other boy at the dance would definitely be looking my way.

My mom walked in. "You look good. Look like I did at your age," she said.

"Tara, my mom's here. I'll call you after the dance."

My mom fixed loose strands of my hair. "Danielle's parents have gotten you two a car."

"Really? Oh my goodness. We're going to be the envy of the school," I said, not bothering to hide my excitement.

Less than thirty minutes later, Danielle rang the doorbell. Her form-fitting sapphire blue dress rocked.

"Come on, girls. Let me take your pictures," my mom said, as she stood behind us.

"We can take some at the dance." I headed toward the door.

"That's fine and dandy, but I want my own personal ones. So come on," my mom insisted.

I looked at Danielle and she looked at me. We knew it was no use in arguing with her. We obeyed because the sooner we took the pictures, the quicker we would be at the dance. My mom took our pictures in various poses in front of the fireplace and outside near our awaiting white long stretch limousine.

Once we were inside the limousine, Danielle poured mineral water in two champagne glasses. We clicked them together as we had seen our parents do at parties.

All eyes were on us when we pulled up in front of the school. We heard people "oohing" and "ah-hing" as the limousine driver opened the door. We exited the limousine like we were superstars. There wasn't a red carpet awaiting us, but we walked up the walkway as if we were preparing for a movie premiere.

Danielle said, "I bet you they wished they'd asked us to the dance now."

"You know they do."

"There goes your boy, Ken, and his date, Lisa."

"Where?" I asked. "So I can make sure I don't look in their direction."

"Keep walking. Don't look to your right."

Danielle and I didn't have an issue finding boys to dance with. It seemed we weren't the only ones at the dance dateless. A lot of the boys were there by themselves. The ones who weren't wished they were there with us, as Danielle and I tore up the dance floor with different guys. Danielle juggled Brad and Michael, plus a few more guys. I had planned on watching her but was too busy taking care of my own business.

By the end of the night, we were counting numbers in the back of the limousine on the ride home. I scrolled through my BlackBerry. "Girl, that was fun. Remind me to go dateless to the next dance."

"From the amount of numbers we got, I doubt we'll be dateless for a while," Danielle responded.

"All we have to do is weed out who has potential and who is a waste of our time."

"Now that's going to be hard. The ones you think are good for you might not be and vice versa."

Danielle had a point. "I guess it'll be trial and error," I replied.

"Let's vow to not get our emotions tied up with any of the dudes until we know for sure what he's about."

"I'll toast to that," I agreed, as our cranberry juice-filled flutes tapped each other, almost spilling on us.

Surprisingly, when I got home my parents were not downstairs waiting on me. The lights beamed from my two little brothers' room. Jay and Jason were one year apart but might as well have been twins because, at ten and eleven years old, they were pests to the third power. I poked my head in their door. Fortunately for me, they were knocked out. Don't get me wrong, they got on my nerves, but I still loved them.

I heard voices coming from down the hall. The closer I got to my parents' room, the louder they got.

"I'm tired of living in Dion McNeil's shadow!" my dad yelled.

"You've never had to live in his shadow," I heard my mom say.

"What's this?" he asked.

I stopped outside of their door. I wondered if I should alert them that I was back at home. My curiosity got the better of me, so I remained outside the door, hoping they didn't open it as they continued to go back and forth.

My mom said, "This is just in case."

"You're keeping an entire scrapbook of this man. What am I supposed to think?"

Dion McNeil, the former NFL star, was hot, but I had no idea my mom was fascinated with the man.

"Trey, please, baby, calm down."

"It's bad enough I have to deal with him being Porsha's father, but this here is ridiculous."

Freeze the frame. *I know my dad did not say what I thought he said.* My mind rewound to his last statement. *Dion McNeil, my dad. What? When and how did this happen?*

I stood frozen outside of my parents' door as their argument continued and my mom basically confirmed the words of the man I had been calling dad for fifteen years.

"Dion never has to know," I heard her say. "I won't renege on my promise."

"Angie, a scrapbook. What if Porsha had found it? What then?"

My mom's voice lowered, so I couldn't hear her response. I put my ear to the door but only heard mumbling. I heard my mom crying, but that was it.

Should I burst through the door and let them know I heard everything. Should I keep the information to myself? How could my parents lie to me all of my life about who my real dad was? How did Dion McNeil end up being my dad? So many questions went through my mind as I stood outside of their door.

I reached out to knock on the door. At the last second, I dropped my hand and walked away.

My night had started on a high note but ended in the gutter.

~ 3 ~

"Porsha, wake up." My mom shook my arm, attempting to wake me up.

"I don't feel good," I responded, turning my back toward her. It wasn't really a lie because my head hurt from crying myself to sleep last night.

My mom placed the back of her hand on my forehead. "You don't feel like you have a fever."

I moaned. "It's my stomach," I lied.

"I'll tell Trey. I have too much stuff to do today, so he'll have to take off work to stay with you."

"Mom, I'm old enough to stay by myself. I just need some Pepto or something, and I'll be all right."

"You sure? I don't like you being in this big old house by yourself."

I turned around and faced her. My tear-swollen eyes made me appear sick. "If I need anything, I'll call you or Dad." As soon as I said the word *Dad*, my head hurt more. I moaned.

"Poor baby." My mom rocked me in her arms. "I have to get the boys ready so I can drop them off at school. You're going to be okay?"

"Yes. Don't worry about me," I assured her, as she got up off my bed and headed out the room. I slid back under the covers.

A few minutes later I heard footsteps approach. "I heard my little princess wasn't feeling too good today," Trey Swint, the man I had known as my father all my life, said.

I couldn't bring myself to face him. I knew if I looked into his face, the floodgates of tears would overflow. Instead, I said, barely above a whisper, "I'll be okay. It's just my stomach."

"If you need me, I'm just a phone call away, okay, dear." He leaned down and kissed me on the cheek. He pulled the covers securely around my shoulders.

"Yes, Daddy." That was it. I couldn't do it. The tears flowed. I was thankful he couldn't see them.

I heard his footsteps as he walked away. I wondered if what I had heard the night before was true. Was Dion McNeil really my father? If so, what was I going to do?

As soon as I heard both cars pull away from the house, I jumped out of bed. I watched my parents drive off to their separate destinations.

Once I was sure they were gone, I rushed to the bathroom to release what I had been holding in for hours. The pathetic-looking girl staring back at me in the bathroom mirror made me want to jump back in bed; instead, I jumped in the shower and stayed there until the water ran cold.

Shivering, I dried off and dressed in a pair of jeans and T-shirt. The suspense of what my mom had been looking at the night before led me to their bedroom.

"Where could it be?" I said out loud as I looked under their bed and fumbled through my mom's side of the dresser drawers. "Jackpot."

A green scrapbook overflowing with newspaper clippings lay hidden beneath her satin nightgown. The next few minutes seemed to move in slow motion as I retrieved the scrapbook and found myself turning the pages as I sat on the edge of my parents' bed.

Staring back at me was a man with my same eyes. I don't know why I hadn't recognized it before, but I was the only one in my family with slanted hazel eyes. Dion McNeil had slanted hazel eyes. Our skin complexion was identical. His smooth caramel complexion matched mine. My parents were from Louisiana, and in our family we came in all shades. It never dawned on me to wonder why both of my parents were mocha chocolate and I came out caramel.

My dad and Dion were in a photo, each holding up an end of the Super Bowl trophy. The caption below the picture, dated two years before I was born, read, "Dallas Cowboys rookies celebrate their first Super Bowl win together."

I skimmed page after page of photos and write-ups of Dion. One photo captured my attention longer than others. A photo of him and his family. The article talked about the reality show surrounding him, his wife, and two daughters. A lightbulb flashed in my head as I recalled watching episodes of the reality show two years ago. My mind couldn't grasp the fact that Dion could be my father, let alone that I might have two half-sisters out there. His other daughter, Jasmine, went to my high school. She and I had a few classes together, but we were far from friends. I didn't like her "I-think-I'm-better-than-you" attitude. I had to go off on her one day. I let Jasmine know her father wasn't the only one who played for the Cowboys. My dad had been a star player too. He didn't need a reality show to keep him in the limelight. After that little confrontation, we'd never seemed to care for each other. We'd been in competition with each other when it came to school activities, and neither one of us could probably think of anything nice to say about the other.

So many questions flashed through my mind. Sort of like a repeat of the night before. How long were my parents going to keep this a secret from me? Why did they keep it a secret from me? Is it because Dion disowned me? Did he even know I existed? My head started pounding. The scrapbook slipped out of my lap and onto the floor.

In between the loud, beating noise in my head, I bent down and picked up the loose pages and stuffed them back in the scrapbook. I hid it back in my mom's dresser drawer. With eyes barely open, I searched my parents' medicine cabinet and found a bottle of aspirin and downed two pills for my headache.

I took a quick glance at myself in the dresser mirror as I left their bathroom and exited back through the bedroom toward my own. I vowed not to look at another mirror anymore on that day. The sound of my cell phone beeping caught my attention as soon as I re-entered my bedroom. I scrolled through several text messages from Danielle and Tara.

For once, I was at a loss for words. What I was going through was too serious to put in a text? I sent them a duplicate message.

Stomach cramps

I tossed the phone on the bed. I lay down, only expecting to spend a few minutes or until the pounding in my head stopped.

The sounds of my little brothers in the hallway woke me up. I couldn't believe I had slept all day. The emotional stress and the lack of sleep from the night before had caught up with me.

"Keep it down," I yelled, as I pulled the covers over my head.

My mom's presence could be felt in the room even before she spoke. Her signature floral fragrance filled the air and seeped under the covers to my nostrils. I turned over and peeped from under the covers.

"You aren't feeling better?" she asked, a concerned look on her face.

I yawned and sat up in bed. "I'm okay. Just tired."

"Take it easy. I called your school and your teachers e-mailed your assignments to you."

Wow! Thanks, Mom. "I'll do it later."

My mom ran her hands through the side of my hair. "You sure you're okay. Your eyes look puffy."

I avoided eye contact. "I'm better. No need to worry about me."

"I can't help but do so. You're my baby girl."

As she talked, all I could think about was the conversation I'd overheard the night before. A conversation I now regretted ever hearing. I guess that's why folks say it's best not to eavesdrop. I could feel a headache returning. I cut her off by saying, "Mom, I better get to working on those assignments. It'll be night before you know it."

"You do that. I need to get dinner ready for tonight." She patted the bed and stood up and left me alone.

I was glad she shut the door. Hopefully, that would keep my two little brothers out of my way. I slid out of the bed and into the desk behind my computer. As they'd promised my mom, some of my teachers had e-mailed me my assignments. Now my head would be pounding for another reason.

One assignment required me to research which presidents were born in the state of Virginia. I didn't have my history book so I clicked on the search engine. Instead of typing in presidents, I typed in the name Dion McNeil.

There were so many hits on his name. I was about to click on some of the links when Jay burst through my door.

"Porsha, Mama wants to see you in her room now," and he stressed the word *now*.

"You better get out of my room," I responded.

"Mom, Porsha's cussing," Jay yelled, as he walked out my room.

"You need to stop lying."

I turned off my computer screen, wondering why my mom wanted to see me.

~ 4 ~

I didn't have to wonder long why my mom had summoned me to her room. As soon as I saw her tear-stained face, I knew something was wrong. She barely raised her head when she spoke. She patted the space beside her on the bed. "Come. Have a seat."

I rushed to the side of the bed. I could now see she was holding a newspaper article of Dion McNeil. Guilt swept across my face when I realized it must have fallen earlier when I was snooping. I thought I had gathered all the papers up and placed them back in the scrapbook, but obviously I hadn't.

We both sat there in silence. Neither one of us knew how to approach the conversation. The sound of the ticking clock seemed to vibrate through the room. I took a quick glance at the clock. My father would be home soon if the time was correct.

My mom reached out and grabbed my hand. "Have you been in my room?" she asked, barely above a whisper.

I could approach the situation two ways: lie or tell the truth. If I lied, things could go on as they were. If I told the truth, then maybe, just maybe I could get the answers to the thousands of questions running through my head. Speaking of heads, the pounding noise that had subsided now returned.

"Porsha, I'm talking to you," her voice got louder as she spoke.

"Yes, ma'am."

"Can you tell me why you were going through my stuff?" she asked, this time in a level voice.

"I—I wanted to find out if what I heard was true," I stuttered.

"Jay, pushed me." Jason ran in the room with a huge scrape on his knee.

"I've told you boys about fighting. I'm going to let your father deal with you two when he gets home."

"It hurts," Jason whined.

"Come on. Let me put some peroxide on it." She stood up off the bed. "Porsha, we're not through, so don't go anywhere," she said to me, as she led Jason into her bathroom to clean the scrape.

When she was done, she kissed Jason on the cheek. "Now, be a good boy and go finish your homework."

"Yes, Mama," Jason said, as he batted his big beautiful black eyelashes.

Instead of returning to the bed, my mom took a seat on her chaise facing the window, in the corner of her bedroom. She looked out the window instead of in my direction. Her voice carried across the room. "I knew this day would come. I was just hoping it wouldn't be like this."

If she expected me to make this easy for her, she could forget it. The feelings of betrayal surfaced, and I wanted answers. I needed answers. I blurted out, "When were you going to tell me Dion McNeil was my father?" There I said it. It was out in the open. No more pretenses.

"I wasn't," my mom admitted.

"You were wrong for keeping this from me."

She turned and faced me. "Me and your dad did what we thought was best."

"For who? You."

"Porsha, there's a lot of stuff you don't know."

I laughed, but it wasn't a happy laugh. "And if it was up to you, I would still be in the dark."

"Dear, please don't be angry with me."

I couldn't believe this. How did she think I should feel? Before I could gather my thoughts together and respond, I heard her ask, "How did you find out?"

"I overheard you and Dad—well, the man I thought was my dad—arguing last night."

My mom was now standing near me. "Trey is still your dad."

"No, he isn't. You lied to me. He lied to me. How could you?"

"Oh, baby." My mother used one of her hands and wiped the tears that I hadn't realized were sliding down my face.

My mom cradled my face in her chest, and I cried like I had never cried before. The kind of cry where tears and snot are mixed together. She rocked me back and forth. I heard Jay call out our mama's name a few times.

"Not now, Jay."

She must have given him one of her "I-mean-business" looks because he didn't argue; instead, I heard his footsteps go in the opposite direction of the room.

My mom brushed my hair with her hands and kept saying, "I'm sorry," over and over.

I heard her words and I wanted to believe them, but something inside of me couldn't immediately accept her apology. My mind flashed back over the last fifteen years of my life. The memories I had shared with my dad were at the forefront. I recalled the father-and-daughter events we attended together. My dad was a victim in all of this just like I was.

I pulled myself out of my mom's grasp and wiped my face with the tissue she handed me.

My dad's voice could be heard in the hallway. My mom said, "Let me talk to your dad first, and then we can continue this discussion after dinner."

Just like that. She dismissed me. Food was the last thing on my mind. I stood up. "I'll pass on dinner." I rushed out the door and bumped into my dad.

"Hold up, baby girl. You feeling better?"

I hugged him tighter than I normally would. "I love you, Daddy." Daddy. *Would he still want me to call him that when he finds out I know the truth?*

"I love you too," he said, giving me a tight hug.

He released me, and I continued to my room. I shut the door. With my back up against the wall, I slid down it until I hit the floor. How would I get past the fact that Trey was not my biological father? My cell phone rang, interrupting my thoughts. I answered it.

"Girl, where have you been?" Danielle said. "I've been calling and texting you all evening."

"I'm dealing with some family drama right now. I'll have to call you back." I didn't give Danielle time to respond. I pressed the end button on my BlackBerry.

Danielle would get an A for persistence because she called back several times. Each time, I pressed the "ignore" button. When the house phone rang, I was sure it was her, so I didn't bother to answer.

Jason yelled from the other end of my door, "Dani's on the phone. She said it's urgent."

"Tell her I'll call her back."

A few seconds later, Jason responded, "She said, you better."

I knew I wouldn't be able to ignore my friends forever, but I needed some "me" time. I closed my eyes, wishing I could erase the last twenty-four hours.

~ 5 ~

I got off the floor and went and sat behind my computer. I turned the screen on. There were several instant messages from Danielle and Tara blinking on my screen. I ignored them all; instead, I clicked on some of the links I had pulled up in the search engine about Dion McNeil.

Wikipedia displayed stats from his NFL career. In fact, his entire professional portfolio filled the page. He'd recently received an award for hosting a show on the Sports Center station. A picture of him with his award and two daughters stared me in the face. I took a closer look at Brenda and Jasmine to see if we resembled each other in any way. Brenda had hazel eyes like me, but Jasmine didn't.

I read their ages again. *Hold the presses. Brenda is several years older than Jasmine. Jasmine is only a year younger than me. That means Dion was sleeping with their mother and my mother at the same time. Oh my goodness, my biological father was a player.*

"Porsha, can we talk?" my mom's voice asked from the other end of my door.

"Coming." I clicked the off button on the computer screen. I took my time walking to the door. I opened up the door expecting to see both of my parents, but my mom was the only one standing on the other end.

"Your dad's downstairs. He thought it would be best if we held this conversation in the den."

I rolled my eyes and walked past her. She did teach me if I didn't have something nice to say, it was best to keep my mouth shut. I was only doing what I was taught. Right now, my mom really didn't want me to tell her how I was feeling. She wouldn't like what I thought about her at this point.

Seeing the pain on my dad's face softened my stance a little. He sat on the sofa with a look of despair on his face. He could barely look me in the face. His eyes were on my mother, who was walking in the room behind me. I took a seat in a chair across from the sofa.

Mom sat next to Dad. She reached for his hand, and I watched their fingers interlock. My dad said, "Angie tells me you found out about your biological father. I want you to know that it doesn't change a thing."

I really wanted to believe him but couldn't. Now that I knew, things were bound to change.

My mom said, "We want you to ask us any questions you may have."

My dad looked in my eyes. "We promise we'll answer them as honestly as we can."

"Are you sure, Dad? Or should I start calling you Trey?"

"Porsha, that's not called for," my mother snapped.

My dad removed his hand. "Angie, let her vent. She has every right."

"She will not disrespect you. You're her father, and she needs to come to terms with it now."

I rolled my eyes and leaned back in my chair. "Are you two through? Because I just got an appetite." Under normal circumstances, I never would have talked to my mom like that, but she needed me to forgive her, not the other way around. I crossed my arms in front of me.

My dad pled, "Porsha, you'll always be my baby girl, so regardless of what happens from this point on, don't you ever forget it."

My heart turned to mush as he spoke. "I have all these questions but don't know where to begin." I normally looked at my mom for assurance, but couldn't bring myself to look her in the eyes.

My dad took over the conversation. "Why don't I tell you how this came about, and Angie can fill in the gaps."

"Fine," I responded.

My mom was a coward. Why wasn't she the one explaining this fiasco, instead of him? The more and more I thought about it, I realized my dad was a saint to take on another man's child as his own.

My mom shifted in her seat. My dad cleared his throat.

She said, "I'll get you something to drink."

"Thanks, dear," he responded, as he cleared his throat again. He faced me as she left the room. "You know this is hurting her just as much as it's hurting you," he said.

"I doubt it." My eyes darted to the floor.

"I'm going to admit this before she comes back. Dion is not my favorite person in the world. You see, believe it or not, him and I used to be best friends. Until, well, until I found out he was sleeping with my woman."

My mom walked back in. "Trey, you could have left that part out."

He took the bottled water from her hand and opened it. "If we're going to tell her the story, she should know the whole story."

"I guess I better be the one to tell her then," my mom said, as she sat beside him and crossed her legs. "What Trey said is true. They were best friends, but when Dion and I hooked up, Trey and I were separated."

My mouth hung open. "So you slept with your husband's best friend? Mom!"

"No, dear. We weren't even married then. We were engaged, and your father was confused about whether or not he wanted to settle down. My heart was hurting. Dion had been a good friend and consoled me."

My dad spat out the water in his mouth. "Hold up. Dion was doing a little bit more than consoling."

She uncrossed her legs. "Fine. He took advantage of my emotional state, and we ended up sleeping together."

"And how old were you?" I asked.

"I was twenty-two years old," she responded. "Young and naïve."

"I'll say," I added.

"Porsha, if this conversation with us is going to work, I suggest you keep your smart aleck comments to a minimum." My mom's eyes locked with mine.

"Needless to say, once I learned what happened, I went and kicked Dion's behind."

"Dear, that's enough," my mom said, as she reached out to touch Dad on the top of his hand.

"Porsha's old enough to hear this. I'm not sugarcoating anything to make Dion look good."

"It's not about making him look good. Anyway, where was I?"

"You said, you were young and naive," I responded.

"Yes. It was only one time, and soon afterward, me and Trey made up and finalized our wedding plans." My mom's eyes glazed over. "Then one of the worst days of my life happened. I found out I was pregnant, and I knew it couldn't be Trey's child because of the timing."

I leaned forward in my chair. "So, you're saying I was a mistake. Oh my God!"

"No, baby. Calm down. You were not a mistake. You were a blessing, and you're still a blessing to me."

"I don't know if I'm ready to hear all of this. Maybe we can finish this talk tomorrow." My hands shook nervously.

My mom looked at my dad and then back at me. "We can talk about this later, whenever you're ready."

I would never be ready, but I didn't say that. "Tomorrow would be better," I said. I stood up and headed for the door.

Before I could reach it, my mom said, "Try to finish your homework. I don't want you to fall behind."

"Whatever," I said, under my breath, but not really caring if she heard me. My whole world as I knew it was crumbling around me. Schoolwork was the last thing on my mind.

~ 6 ~

The next morning I continued to give my mother major attitude. How could she keep something as important as my biological father from me?

"Porsha, you'll eventually have to talk to me. The silent treatment is not going to work," my mom said, as she attempted to hold a conversation with me.

I ignored her while I ate my bowl of cereal. The tension in the kitchen was thick. Jay and Jason, being their normal selves, got on my nerves.

My dad or Trey or whatever I would end up calling him walked into the kitchen. "Porsha, if you like, I can drop you off at school today."

He didn't have to say it twice. I jumped up from the table. "Let me grab my backpack."

I placed my earphones to my iPod in my ear as my dad pulled out of the driveway. I looked up toward the house just in time to catch my mom standing in the doorway. A part of me felt sorry for her, but the pain she was feeling, she brought on herself. Maybe, she'll think twice about keeping major secrets from me or anyone else.

"Baby girl, let's talk for a minute," Trey said, as he pulled out on the major street leading to my school.

I removed the earpiece from my ear and gave him my full attention. "I'm listening."

"In my heart, you are mine. I've loved you from the moment I knew you were conceived."

Wow! He was special to love someone else's seed. That's why I loved him so much. I didn't want to lose his love. Trey would always be my daddy. I just hoped he would continue to feel the same love for me, even if I decided to reach out to Dion.

"I love you too, Daddy. Is it all right for me to still call you Daddy?"

"Baby girl, it would hurt me if you stopped calling me Daddy," he responded.

I could hear the fear in his voice. "You'll always be my daddy, no matter what," I assured him.

His frown was replaced with a slight smile. "That's good to know. I also wanted you to know if you want to reach out to Dion, I will understand."

"I'm not so sure about doing that."

"Whatever you decide, I support your decision. I will not stand in your way of getting to know your biological father."

By now we were near my school. My heart was breaking all over again because with his words, I could see the pain of uncertainty in his eyes. I didn't know what to say to reassure him. We rode the rest of the way to school in silence.

"I love you, Daddy," I said, while fidgeting with my backpack.

"Love you too, baby girl," he responded, as he watched me exit his SUV.

We waved good-bye to each other right before I walked up the sidewalk toward the school. I looked back, and he was still parked. I waved once more and headed toward the front door.

Ken's face was the last one I wanted to see, but he rushed up to me as soon as he saw me walk down the hallway.

"Porsha, we need to talk," he stated, as he blocked my path.

"Another time, but right now, I'm not in the mood."

Ken reached for my arm, and I jerked it.

"I'm sorry, okay. I was a fool," he blurted out.

That he was, but I had too much going on and wasn't in the mood for his theatrics. "Save your apology for someone who cares. Now move, because I have to go to class." By now, I was standing with my arms folded and my head tilted to the side with pouted lips.

"I'm not giving up on us," he said, as he moved out of my way.

"Don't bother," I responded, and kept walking to my first period class.

Mr. Trudeau asked for my assignment as soon as I entered the door.

"I didn't get it," I lied.

I would continue to tell that lie to all of my teachers that day. Instead of working out during gym, my gym teacher allowed me to spend the time catching up on my schoolwork. After gym came the hour I dreaded—lunch time. I would no longer be able to avoid questioning from Danielle and Tara.

Both of my BFFs were seated in the lunch room when I arrived. I didn't have much of an appetite, so I grabbed some fruit and juice and headed their way.

"Look who showed up," Tara teased.

"I've had a lot going on."

Danielle barely said a word.

Tara continued, "You've been ignoring us for days now, but that's okay. We understand."

"Well, I don't," Danielle snapped.

"Dani, I thought we agreed not to say anything," Tara said.

"Porsha, what is going on with you? And we want to know now."

If my head wasn't about to burst with all of the information and tension inside, I would have made them wait, but I needed to talk to someone.

While peeling my orange, I spilled my guts. "My dad's not my father. Dion McNeil is," I blurted out.

Danielle laughed. "You're trying to punk us."

Tara added, "Yes, come on now. Be for real."

"I'm telling y'all the truth. *The* Dion McNeil is my biological father."

Danielle and Tara looked at each other, and then both sets of eyes were back on me.

Tara broke the silence. "Wow! So how long have you known?"

I recounted how I found out.

Danielle interrupted, "So your mom kept a secret like this from you? Wait until I tell my mom."

I shook my head. "Don't tell your mom anything we discussed here. In fact, don't neither one of y'all tell anyone what I told you."

"Well, it's just my mom," Danielle said.

"I don't care. I'm only telling you this because you're my best friends." I knew Danielle wouldn't be able to keep it from her mom, but I could at least throw in the friendship card to persuade her to hold off on disclosing it to her mother.

Tara, the more reasonable-sounding out of the two today, asked, "So when are you going to meet your real father?"

"Good question. I don't know. To be truthful to you, I really don't think he knows I exist."

"But what if he does and he just allowed your parents to raise you? What then?" Danielle asked.

I shrugged my shoulders. "I don't know. I haven't thought about it. Besides, I'm not sure if I'm going to reach out to him or not. My life's perfect just the way it is."

"Speaking of perfect . . . there goes someone who thinks she's perfect," Tara said, as she looked toward the front door of the cafeteria.

My eyes darted in the same direction. There standing near the door was my archenemy, also now known as my half-sister, Ms. Jasmine McNeil. Dion McNeil's daughter. The daughter he seemed to dote on. The daughter he gave all of his love to while ignoring me.

~ 7 ~

I agreed to call Danielle and Tara later as we parted ways after lunch. The remaining part of my day dragged on. I barely paid attention to my teachers. I even flunked a pop quiz because I hadn't read the assignment. Normally, I would be concerned with keeping my 4.0 average, but my grades were the furthest thing from my mind.

When the last bell rang ending school for the day, instead of feeling relief, I felt fearful of what was to come next. My mom's car sat near the curb. I walked extra slow. She spoke when I opened the door, but I didn't respond.

"Porsha, we can't go on like this," she said, as she waited for me to put on my seatbelt.

"Hi, Mom," I said loudly. I looked her directly in the face. "Is that better?"

"Dear, I know this is a difficult time for you, but don't forget your place. I'm still your mother, and I will not be tolerating any more of your attitudes."

I rolled my eyes and looked out the window as she pulled away from the school. Music and the fast rate of my heartbeat were the only two things I heard as we rode the way home in silence. She barely had the car parked before I jumped out of the car. I fumbled through my backpack for my keys but without success.

"Here," my mom said, as she handed me her house keys.

I turned the lock and handed them back to her. Without waiting for her to say anything else, I made a beeline to my bedroom. I threw my backpack on the floor and then plopped down on my bed. I leaned back and closed my eyes. My hopes of relaxing were dashed when my mom burst in my room without knocking.

"We need to talk," she said.

I responded, "I don't feel like talking."

My mom walked to the bed and sat down. "Sit up, so we can talk."

I grudgingly sat up. "I'm all talked out."

"Good. Then you can listen."

My mom was determined to talk, so I gave her my undivided attention. "I'm listening."

With a faraway look in her eyes, she said, "I love your father."

"Which one?" I asked.

"Trey is your father and will always be your father as far as I'm concerned," she responded.

"Then why were you keeping a scrapbook then?" I asked.

"Just in case. But I never knew 'just in case' would actually happen. I never meant for you to find out the way that you did."

I chuckled. "I don't think you ever meant for me to find out, period."

My mom looked down. "You're not far from the truth."

I could feel the rage inside of me return. "Mother, dear, what is the truth? I want the whole truth and nothing but the truth."

"Maybe we should wait for Trey to get here."

Oh, no. She was not going to get off that easy. I could see her chickening out. "Mama, I need you to tell me what happened. I can't wait for Trey. I need answers now."

"Don't ever disrespect Trey again by calling him by name. He's your dad . . . your father . . . your guardian. He's done more for you than Dion would have ever done."

My mom actually sounded like I had made her mad. Did I care? No. She owed me answers, and I wanted them. Right now, we were at a standstill. We each stared at the other without saying a word.

When I didn't back down but just blinked my eyes a few times, my mom went on to say, "Dion and I were never a couple. Truthfully, I regretted the moment we slept together because I was also friends with his wife."

"How could you do that to one of your friends?" I asked. *Skank* was the only word I could think of. I felt ashamed that I equated that word with my mother.

"Dion was having problems at home. Your dad . . . Trey, was out doing his thing. I thought he didn't love me. I was confused. I needed to feel loved, and Dion, for just that one night, made me feel loved."

"Mom, I never knew you to be so insecure." I wasn't liking the things coming out of my mouth toward my mom, but I was still upset.

"Dear, my patience is getting thin, so I suggest you keep your smart aleck comments to yourself."

I retreated. My mom was from Shreveport, Louisiana and told me plenty of stories of how her parents disciplined her. I had gone fifteen years without receiving any whuppings, so I wasn't about to start now.

She continued with her story. "Your dad and I reconciled, and as we were saying to you, that's when I found out I was pregnant."

"Tell me this. Does Dion know he's my father?" I asked with clenched fists.

"Dion suspected you were his, but when Trey agreed to be your father, I lied and told Dion you weren't his."

A sense of relief swept through me. I think that was one of my biggest fears. Knowing that he really didn't know I existed made me feel so much better. I think I was more afraid that he knew about me but chose to disown me than anything. "So, you're the reason why me and my real father were kept apart? How could you, Mom?"

Shame disclosed in her eyes, my mom responded, "I did what I thought would be best for you. Trey has been a good husband to me and father to you."

"No, Mom, you did what was best for you," I snapped. "You didn't want to lose Dad, so you took the easy route."

I guess I must have hit home because my mom didn't disagree. She didn't even raise her voice.

"Yes, I admit, I was a coward. I couldn't face Dion's wife. I didn't want to break up his family. And, yes, I wanted to hold on to Trey too."

"Wow! I guess I inherit keeping secrets from you. I've never been one to tell anyone else's secrets."

"I'm wrong for not telling you. I hope one day you'll forgive me," my mom said, as she stood up.

"Maybe one day, I will, but right now, Mom, this is a lot to digest." If she was looking for me to ease her guilty conscience, she was out of luck.

"Honey, I'm home," I heard my dad say from somewhere in the distance.

"I'm in Porsha's room," Mom yelled out.

My dad walked in and looked like he had the weight of the world on his shoulders. "Good. I'm glad you're both here. I have something to tell you."

I slid to the edge of the bed.

My mom said, "What, baby? Just tell us."

My dad looked directly at me when he said, "I contacted Dion. He's coming over this weekend so we can all talk."

"Did you tell him about Porsha?" my mom asked.

"No. We'll tell him together. He'll be here Saturday afternoon. Just thought you two should know."

"That's tomorrow," I responded.

"You should have talked to me before you did that," my mom said.

My dad responded, "Fifteen years ago, I let you do what you thought was best for Porsha. As man of this house, I'm now doing what I think is best for Porsha."

"But—" my mom said.

"No buts. This secret has gone on long enough. It's time for this secret to be told."

Without saying another word, both of my parents left me to ponder this new chain of events.

~ 8 ~

I tossed and turned in my sleep the majority of the night. The thought of meeting Dion McNeil weighed heavily on my mind.

My mom walked around in a zombie-like state last night and today. I convinced her to let me go to the mall with Danielle and Tara. I figured she would be glad to get rid of me as she dealt with her own thoughts.

"How do you like this on me?" Tara asked, as she puckered out her lips, showcasing the hot pink lip gloss.

"That color is too bright," Danielle responded.

I agreed.

Tara picked up a tissue and wiped it off. "How about this one?" she asked, this time rubbing on cherry red lip gloss.

"That's much better," I responded.

"I prefer this chocolate bronze myself," Danielle said, as she lifted the tube off the lip gloss tester and applied it.

"Perfect," I responded. "I might try that one myself."

Danielle got the attention of the sales clerk. "We want two chocolate bronzes and one cherry red."

Less than fifteen minutes later, we were leaving the department store with our purchases. Danielle and Tara were happy to participate in my retail therapy as we went from store to store. By the time Danielle's mom picked us up, we all had dozens of shopping bags.

"I hate to see my bill next month," Danielle's mom said, as she opened up the trunk of her luxury car. It was easy to spot Danielle's mom with her curly honey-blond shoulder-length hair.

"Mom, I get an allowance. It's not like it's costing you anything extra," Danielle responded.

"Anyway, glad you girls had fun."

We listened to Danielle's mom talk about shopping and how we should appreciate all of the advantages we had because, when she was growing up, her parents couldn't afford to keep her in designer clothes. I could tell her story in my sleep because she never let any of us forget where she came from.

By the time we reached my house, I was thrilled to be getting out of the car. "Thanks, Mrs. Davis,"

I said, as I gathered my bags and said my good-byes to my friends.

No one was home when I got there. I went straight to my room and tried to put away the items I bought before my parents returned. I too got an allowance, but my purchases put me over my monthly allowance. I knew when my dad got the bill, he would be complaining. Normally, all I would have to do is bat my pretty eyes and he would stop the lecture. I wasn't sure what his reaction would now be.

I glanced at the clock. Four o'clock was quickly approaching. The doorbell rang, and my parents were nowhere in sight. I glanced out my window and saw a car parked outside that I didn't recognize. The doorbell rang again.

It must be him. I rushed to the bottom of the stairs. I took a few deep breaths before looking through the peephole. There he stood. My biological father. He looked just as handsome in person as he did on the television.

His back was turned when I opened the door. He turned around to face me. "Hello there. I was just about to leave," his baritone voice said, acknowledging me.

"My, uh, parents will be here in a minute," I stuttered.

"I can wait in my car until they come," he responded.

If he wasn't my father, I would have agreed. He was no stranger. He was Dion McNeil. He was my father. "You can wait in the living room. I'll call my dad to let them know you're here." I moved to the side and allowed him inside the house. I gently closed the door behind him.

"Which way is the living room?" he asked.

He probably thought I was a dunce, from the way I was acting. "Follow me," I responded. "Have a seat," I said, as I moved out of his way. "I'll be right back."

I dialed my mom's number. "Where are y'all? He's here," I said, barely above a whisper.

"Where is he now?" she asked.

"He's in the living room."

"You let that man in my house without us being there. Porsha, you shouldn't have done that," she snapped.

"It's not like he's a mass murderer or anything. He's my father."

"Shh. Before he hears you. Now you go back upstairs. Tell him we'll be there in about five minutes. We had to drop off Jay and Jason for their overnight slumber party," my mom responded before disconnecting the call.

I wondered where they were. Good. My night would be brat-free with the two of them gone. I walked back to the living room and stood in the entryway for a few seconds. Before I could open my mouth to say anything, Dion said, "You're just as beautiful as your mom."

I blushed. "Thanks. Mom said they would be here in five minutes."

"What school are you going to?" he asked.

"Plano High."

"Really? So does my daughter Jasmine. You two are around the same age, so maybe you know her."

"I know of her, but we're not friends."

"Maybe, after today, we can change that."

I shrugged my shoulders. There was an awkward silence.

Dion broke it. "Where's your bathroom?"

"It's down the hallway to the right." I pointed in the direction of the bathroom.

I remained standing in the doorway as he went to use the bathroom. Five minutes had long passed, so where were my parents? I really needed them to hurry up. I didn't know how much longer I could talk to him without bombarding him with a lot of questions. I needed to know how he felt about me being his daughter. I needed answers.

And, before the day was over, I planned on getting them.

~ 9 ~

It took my parents an extra fifteen minutes to get home. I knew because I was watching the clock. I decided to leave Dion in the living room by himself with his thoughts while I sat in the foyer waiting for my parents' arrival.

My mom rushed through the door. "Dear, where is he?" she asked.

"He's in the living room. What took y'all so long?" I asked.

"Traffic, baby," my dad responded. "Go upstairs. One of us will come get you when we're ready."

I pouted. They were both too anxious to notice that I hadn't retreated up the stairway. I watched them enter the living room hand in hand. Then I tiptoed closer to the living room door so I could hear, being careful not to expose myself.

"Well, hello, Dion," my dad said.

"Trey. Angie."

"Dion," my mom responded.

There was an awkward silence.

I moved closer and peeked in the room. Everyone's back was toward the door so no one noticed I was there.

My dad cleared his throat. "I'm sure you're wondering why I called you here today."

Dion responded, "You did catch me off guard. We were friends once so I'm here."

My mom said, "This isn't about your friendship. This is more important."

"There's no easy way to say this, so I'll just tell you," my dad said.

"Trey, you aren't dying, are you? Man, I'm sorry. We can brush our past under the rugs. I'm here for you, man, if you need me," Dion said, concern in his voice.

I heard my dad say, "No, man. I'm in perfect health."

Dion's head switched in the direction of my mother. "Angie?"

"It's about our daughter Dion. You and I have a daughter," my mom blurted.

"Say what?" he asked.

My dad added, "What Angie is trying to say is, remember the time you and her cheated? Well, you left her with a package."

Dion stuttered, "It can't be. We used a condom."

"Apparently, it broke," my dad snapped.

"Hey, man. I told you back then I'm sorry. I had no idea."

"Well, now you know," my mom said.

"If it was up to me, you never would have known," my dad confided.

"This is a lot to digest. I'm wondering, why now? Why after all these years are you telling me now? Why not then? Why should I believe you?" Dion blurted out question after question.

My mom responded, "Like Trey said, if it was up to us, you wouldn't be sitting here right now. Our daughter found out about you, and Trey thought it was best that you know now. This will give you the opportunity to build a relationship with your daughter . . . that is, if you want to."

"Look, this is a lot to digest. We need to do blood tests. I'll need to speak with my attorney," he said.

"Other than Trey, you were the only man I had slept with during a two-year period, so Dion, without a doubt, you are my daughter's biological father."

The tension in the air was thick. Dion's voice sounded frustrated instead of relaxed like earlier. "You can't just drop a bomb on me like this and think I'm going to take your word for it. You've been lying for fifteen years. Why should I believe you now?"

My dad said, "Get the DNA test, but in the meantime, I need for you to figure out what you're going to do about my daughter."

"According to Angie, you mean my daughter, right?" Dion said. His head seemed to be looking directly at my dad.

"Dion, don't get it twisted. Porsha Marie Swint will ALWAYS be my daughter. And it's my love for her that prompted me to contact you."

"I'm just saying. If it's proven she's my daughter, we're going to have to do a name change. A lot of things will change."

My mom responded, "Porsha's a Swint in every sense of the word, so you can forget that."

Dion said, "Look, I don't want to fight with you, Angie, but right now, I don't think you have a leg to stand on. You kept my daughter away from me."

My dad interrupted him. "You will not disrespect my wife. She did—we did what we thought was best for all of us. You were married. We were getting married. We didn't find out the child wasn't mine until after she was born. By then, I, yes, I felt it best to leave things the way they were. I've loved Porsha since she was in her mom's belly."

Tears streamed down my face as I listened to my dad express his unconditional love for me as if I was his biological daughter. I loved him too. I was confused about how I should feel about Dion. He kept asking for a blood test. I don't know why he wouldn't take my mom's word for it. She had no reason to lie to him now.

Dion responded, "Trey, I'm sure you love her. And, if she's mine, in due time, I'm sure I'll love her too."

What does he mean, "if she's mine"? My mom just told you I'm your daughter. Dude, you're in denial. I felt like screaming, but I wasn't supposed to be downstairs overhearing their conversation. Eavesdropping wasn't something I normally did, although, lately, you couldn't tell.

My mom said, "She's yours. So make whatever arrangements you need to make. You're not the only one with attorneys."

"This is a lot to dump on someone. How am I supposed to feel? You've kept secrets and now think I'm supposed to believe whatever y'all tell me. Come on now."

"I was going to have Porsha come back downstairs, so we could make the official introduction, but based on your reaction, I don't think it's a good idea," my dad responded.

I started to back up and accidentally hit the table near the wall. *Busted.*

"Porsha, is that you?" my mom shouted out.

"Yes, it's me," I responded. I walked and stood in the middle of the doorway.

"I thought I told you to go upstairs," my dad said.

I stuttered, "Well, what had happened was—"

My mom said, "Dear, go back upstairs. We'll talk later."

I looked at Dion to see if he was going to say anything. To my disappointment, he didn't. Feeling rejected, I hung my head low and this time did what my parents had originally advised me. I headed upstairs to my bedroom.

~ 10 ~

I paced back and forth in my room. I peeped out the window to see if Dion had left, but his car remained outside. The anticipation of what else was happening downstairs kept me on pins and needles. The knock on the door startled me.

"Porsha, can I come in?" my mom asked.

"Sure." Regardless of my response she was going to enter anyway, so it really didn't matter what I said.

"How much did you overhear?" she asked, as she entered the room.

I shrugged my shoulders. "So, is he gone?" I asked.

"No, he wants to talk to you before he leaves."

"Really," I responded. I was surprised. "I thought he wanted to wait until after the DNA test."

"So you did hear. I've told you about eaves-dropping."

"It wasn't like I was trying to eavesdrop. You guys weren't whispering."

My mom placed her arm around my shoulders. "If you're not ready, I will tell him, it'll have to be another time. I don't want you to do anything you're not ready to do."

When I felt her arms around my shoulders, I wanted to lay my head on her shoulder and cry. I was confused. I didn't know what I should do. A part of me wished things could go back to the day before I found out Trey was not my biological father. "I'll talk to him. It's not like I haven't talked to him before."

"Are you sure? Because we can set up another meeting," she said.

I think Mom really wanted me to wait to meet him for her own selfish reasons. "Let's get this over with."

I pushed back my insecurities and decided to venture down the stairs behind my mom. After all the drama, I was now face to face with the man who now knew I was his daughter.

My parents both stood by the fireplace.

Dion seemed to examine my face, probably trying to see if there was any resemblance. "You have my eyes," he said. He patted the cushion next to him on the sofa. "Come. Sit."

I glanced over at my parents, who were still standing by the fireplace. My dad nodded his head up and down. I took that as encouragement and I hesitantly did as I was told.

"You're a beautiful young lady," Dion said.

"Thanks," I responded.

"I wanted you to know, if you're my daughter, I want us to get to know each other better."

My mind held on to the word *if*. I blurted, "I *am* your daughter. My mom confirmed it."

"I know, dear. But I just want to make sure before—"

I interrupted him. "Before what? Before you start dishing out money? I don't need your money. My dad has money."

"Porsha, I didn't mean to upset you."

My dad walked over. "Dion, I think it's best that you go now. When you're ready to accept Porsha as your daughter, maybe we can try this again."

"That's okay, Dad. I want to hear what Dion has to say." I stretched the word *Dion*.

"Porsha, I'm sorry. I didn't mean to hurt your feelings," Dion said.

I folded my arms and leaned back on the sofa. "I'm not so sure I want to get to know you anyway. I have a dad."

"If you're mine, I want us to have a relation-ship."

"There goes that word *if* again. I AM your daughter, but like I said, I already have a dad, so please don't feel obligated." I shifted my body, so my back was now turned toward him.

My dad said, "Dion, man, please leave. Call us when you set up the DNA test, and Angie and Porsha will be there."

Dion remained seated for a minute. I could feel his eyes on me. "Porsha, I will see you later."

"Uh-huh," I responded. I felt him get off the couch.

"I'll walk you out," my dad said.

My mom rushed to my side. "Are you all right?"

"My moms kept secrets from me, and my real father doesn't want to acknowledge I'm his. How do you think I feel?" I jumped off the couch and ran upstairs as the tears flowed down my face, staining my shirt.

I threw myself on the bed and sobbed like a baby.

My dad came into the room and took me in his arms as I cried in his arms. "Baby girl, it's going to be all right," he said, as he rocked me back and forth.

"He doesn't want me. I'm glad he didn't know I was his."

My dad looked me in the eyes. "It's not that, sweetheart. He just found out about you. He's just being cautious and wants to make sure before getting emotionally attached."

"Well, I hate him, and I don't want anything else to do with him. You're all the dad I need."

"You don't mean that."

"Yes, I do," I responded.

"I can't believe I'm saying this, because Dion is still not one of my favorite people, but give him a chance. The DNA tests will be done soon, and he'll come to terms that you're his."

"I don't want to be his. I want things the way they were."

"Awe, sweetheart, it's going to be all right. Like I've told you before, you will always be my baby girl." He continued to rock me back and forth.

My mom stood in the doorway. For the first time since the day she discovered I knew the truth, I saw tears stream down her face. She wrapped her arms around herself.

My dad brushed the hair out of my face and kissed me on the forehead. "We're going to get through this. Love you. Get you some rest, and if you need to talk, you know where to find us."

They closed the door behind them, and I was left to my thoughts. I fell back on the bed and stared at the ceiling. Each time I closed my eyes, I saw visions of my real father and replayed our short conversation over and over in my head.

Once he confirmed I was his via the DNA test, what then? Where would we go from here? What would my little brothers think when they found out? How was my life going to change? Those questions and more swam around in my head before I drifted off to sleep.

Normally, my Sunday consisted of going to church and spending time with my family, but this Sunday my parents and I slept in. Well, they may have slept, but I tossed and turned and had a restless night of sleep and had the bags under my eyes to prove it.

Frustrated, I gave up on going back to sleep. I dialed Danielle's number. "I met Dion yesterday," I said.

"How did it go?" she asked.

"Let me get Tara on the phone so I can tell you both at the same time." I placed Danielle on hold and added Tara in on the call.

I recounted what occurred. "So now we're waiting on the DNA test."

"Wow! This is so exciting. Dion McNeil is your dad. That's just way cool," Danielle said.

"I wish he wasn't. I love my dad. I don't need another one."

Tara said, "I wished mine would come around more."

We listened to Tara go on and on about how she felt about not seeing her father. I welcomed the temporary distraction from my own problems. My phone clicked. I saw a number I didn't recognize. "Hold on, y'all," I said, right before clicking over.

"I wanted to check on you," a familiar voice said from the other end.

"Kenneth?" I asked.

"Yes, Porsha. You seemed out of it at school."

"Look, I don't have time for drama. My life is complicated as it is," I responded.

"But I like you. I thought you liked me too."

"I did. But that was before I saw you liking all those other girls."

"They don't mean anything to me. I want you to be my girl."

Kenneth sounded so sexy when he said it. I forgot about my two BFFs being on the other end of the phone. "Ken, I don't know. You seem to have too much going on."

"Porsha, I'm not giving up on you that easily. I want you, and I know you want me too."

"Give it up, Ken. I don't have time for the games. Got to go. I have someone on the other end of my phone."

I clicked over and told Danielle and Tara about the conversation with Kenneth.

Tara said, "He's something else. I wouldn't give him time of day."

"I wish it was that easy. He's such a cutie."

"Yes, he is," Danielle agreed.

"Looks aren't everything," Tara said.

Danielle and I said in unison, "Yes, they are."

"Y'all are so shallow."

I continued the playful banter with my two BFFs. Talking to them made me feel better. I felt energized and could face whatever happened next.

My appetite returned, so after showering and getting dressed, I went downstairs to fix myself something to eat.

I heard my parents arguing. The sound was coming from the kitchen. Once again, I found myself eavesdropping.

"This is all your fault," I heard my mom say.

"Look . . . she deserves to know her biological father. Do you think this is easy on me? No, it isn't," my dad said, as I saw him approach my mom and wrap his arm around her waist.

"This is tearing me apart. What if, after he gets confirmation, he doesn't want to have anything to do with her? That would break her heart and mine."

"He will have to deal with me. I'm not going to let anyone hurt Porsha."

Tired of eavesdropping, I made my presence known. "Hi. Didn't know y'all were down here." I went in search of a saucer so I could make a sandwich.

"If you can wait about twenty minutes, lunch will be here. We ordered from your favorite Italian restaurant," my mom said, releasing herself from my dad's embrace.

"Cool," I responded. I continued to the refrigerator and poured myself a drink.

Thirty minutes later, my parents and I were enjoying a nice lunch. My mom's cell phone ringing interrupted our quiet family time.

"That was Jay," she said after hanging up. "They are ready for us to come pick them up. You want to go with us? We were going to swing by the park."

"No, I think I'll stay around the house and chill," I responded.

I spent the afternoon by myself surfing the Internet. So many questions popped up in my head about Dion McNeil. I wanted to know everything about him. I wanted to know if some of the mannerisms I had mimicked any of his. I wondered, once he got the test results he insisted on getting, would he embrace me as his daughter? Or would he keep me at arm's length?

I found myself reading article after article about Dion McNeil. I clicked on a few video links from the reality show he and his family did one year. The interaction between him and his other daughters, Brenda and Jasmine, seemed to be solid. Out of the two, Jasmine appeared to be a spoiled brat. Brenda seemed more laid-back.

I wondered how they would react when they found out about me. I wondered how I would react if my dad came home and said he had another child. I didn't think I would like it. But from the information I read on the Internet, their parents were no longer together, so it shouldn't be a big deal. Brenda was about twenty, so my guess was, she was in college. I'd always wanted an older sister, but never thought it would be like this.

I logged on to my Facebook account. I went back and forth in my mind if I should send friend requests to Brenda and Jasmine. I wasn't sure if they knew about me by now or not. After careful consideration, I sent a friend request to Brenda. Then I started to do the same to Jasmine but decided against it.

Speaking of Jasmine, I would love to be a fly on the wall when she finds out I am her half-

sister. I chuckled out loud. Maybe being Dion's child wouldn't be too bad after all. Jasmine needed to be brought down a peg or two, and I would be just the girl to do it.

~ 12 ~

Monday morning came quick. I'd had a good night's rest, so I wasn't groggy. Jason's and Jay's annoying habits didn't get on my nerves like they normally did. My dad dropped me off at school, and I went to class as if life was normal.

In between second and third period I received a text message from my mom alerting me that she would be checking me out early. Dion moved fast. He already had a DNA test scheduled for later on that afternoon.

During lunch, I remained quiet while I listened to Danielle and Tara talk.

Danielle said, "We need to start planning your party?"

"What party?" I asked.

Tara said, "Your sweet sixteen. It's in less than a month, and we need to get your invitations out."

"Bah. That's the last thing on my mind right now."

"Well, let's get it back on your mind," Danielle said.

"I'll have to talk to my parents. They might not want to give me a party now." I thought I would be more excited about turning sixteen. I didn't want to disappoint my two BFFs, but I wasn't in a partying mood.

"Ask your mom today, so we'll know how many people we can invite," Tara said.

"Uh-oh. Look whose coming this way." Danielle pointed.

Kenneth approached our table. "Hi, Porsha."

Danielle cleared her throat. "Is that all you see here?"

"Ladies."

"Whatever, Ken. You're so fake," Tara said.

"And you're so invisible to me."

"You don't have to insult my friends." I looked up in Ken's face.

"I'm sorry. Will you forgive me?" he asked.

"Maybe, but for now, I'm talking to my friends. I'll talk to you later." I looked away and started talking to Danielle again.

Kenneth left the table in a huff, but I didn't care. He was yesterday's news. Even if I wasn't dealing with family issues, he wasn't going to get my full attention ever again.

"Ken won't let up on you, will he?" Tara asked, between bites.

"He might as well. There are too many other boys interested in me, and they don't come up with all his drama."

Danielle said, "Boys are nothing but drama, some less than others."

I shook my head. "I guess you're right."

My cell phone vibrated. It was Kenneth sending me a text message. I looked up in his direction, and he waved. I looked back down at my phone and hit the delete button. I placed my phone back in my pocket. "On to the next one."

"That's what I'm talking about," Tara said, giving me a high-five.

"Speaking of next, look who just walked in the cafeteria," Danielle said.

All three sets of eyes turned and looked. Standing before us was the boy who I used to have a crush on, Cole Baylor, or C.B., as I heard some of his friends say. He was Plano High's star basketball player, and rumor had it that the NBA reps were looking at him. I forgot about all of my woes and smiled. He smiled too. I wasn't sure if the smile was meant for me, but it felt like it was. Standing over six feet, his teen body was not lanky but built. He reminded me of Trey Songz, the R & B singer, except he was taller and younger.

Tara and Danielle were talking, but I was entranced by the sight of Cole. For the first time since finding out Dion was my father, my mind was on something else.

"He's coming this way," I interrupted them.

My heartbeat increased. Sweat started to form on my forehead. Everything seemed to move in slow motion. All three of us sat there silent, hoping and wishing he was headed to our table. He was steps away.

I didn't know which one of us he would speak to first, but I crossed my fingers and hoped it was me. *Breathe*, I told myself over and over, the closer he got.

"Hi, ladies," he said, as he approached our table.

We all responded in low voices. A hush seemed to sweep the area where we sat as I noticed how some of the other girls at the surrounding tables were watching us.

"Do you mind if I take a seat?" he asked.

"No, of course not," Danielle took the liberty of speaking for all of us.

He grabbed a chair from another table and placed it in between Danielle and me. Tara's face showed disappointment. Now, it was down to me and Danielle. Most guys would go for Danielle, so when he turned and asked me if he

could have my phone number, talk about surprised.

I exhaled and glanced at Danielle but didn't
say a word.

Danielle said, "If she doesn't give you her
number, I will. Her number is 972-555-4959."

Cole entered my number in his phone. "I'll be
calling you," he said, as he exited the table.

Oh my goodness. Cole left me speechless.
Right now I was the envy of all of the girls, including my two BFFs.

"I hope you say more than a few words to him
when he calls you," Danielle said, snapping me
out of my trance.

"I can't believe he wanted my number. Thanks,
Dani, for rescuing me. I couldn't speak. It's like I
had a frog in my throat or something."

"That's what friends are for. Although, I must
admit, I thought he was coming over here to talk
to me. But if it couldn't be me, I'm glad it was
you."

Tara said, "But what about me?"

"If it couldn't be me or Porsha, it would have
been good if it was you."

They went back and forth.

My cell phone vibrated. I looked at the text
message. The sight of Cole's message put a smile
on my face.

~ 13 ~

Daydreaming about Cole got me through the rest of my school day. I got excused from class when the office notified my teacher that my mom was there to check me out. I hurried out of the room to meet my mom, who was waiting near the front door.

"I'm sorry, I'm late, but traffic was a mess as usual," my mom said.

"Perfect. Because the teacher was about to put on some boring video. I probably would have fallen asleep anyway."

While driving to the doctor's office, my mom asked, "Do you have any questions for me?"

"Will the procedure take long?" I had no idea what a DNA test would entail.

"All the doctor is going to do is swab your mouth and put it in a tube. Then you and I will be on our merry way."

"That's it? I'm getting checked out of school for that? I could have used a Q-tip and gave it to you and stayed in school."

My mom looked at me with a raised eyebrow. "When have you ever had a problem with being checked out of school? I tell you." She shook her head.

Under normal circumstances, I would have been overjoyed, but not for this occasion. Not to prove to a man who avoided the obvious, that I, Porsha Marie Swint, was his daughter. Once he did find out, what next? That was the million-dollar question.

The waiting room was packed when we arrived at the doctor's office. I wondered why some of the other people were here. Snotty-nosed kids were running around. I was hoping none came near me. I didn't want to get sick from any of their germs.

While my mom filled out the paperwork the receptionist handed her, I flipped through pages of one of the latest fashion magazines. Still bored, I turned on my phone and decided to text Danielle and Tara to let them know where I was. Once I was finished texting, I surfed the Web and read up on the latest entertainment gossip. I chuckled at some of the crazy stories posted.

Thirty minutes later, we were called to go to the patient's waiting room. The walk down the hallway would change my life forever.

Although my mom had explained it would be a simple procedure, I still found myself shaking a little as the doctor entered the room.

"Hello, ladies. This shouldn't take long at all."

I listened intently as the doctor explained to us what he was going to do.

Once the swab test was done on the both of us, we were excused to leave.

Dion entered the premises as we were walking out. He spoke, and I spoke back.

My mom said, "Our part is done. We expect to hear from you by the end of the week."

"I'm paying to have the results back in three days, so you'll hear from me then," he responded. Without saying another word, he continued toward the doctor's office.

"That man is something else. I hate he's back in our lives," my mom mumbled.

I began to wonder if there was more behind my mom's anger than she was letting on. She did sleep with him to conceive me, so there had to be something there. I took the opportunity on the ride home to probe. "Mom, how did you feel about Dion, you know, before me?" I asked.

"Dion, was all right. He was Trey's friend. He spent a lot of time at the house. Back then, me and your father was living together. When we broke up, Trey left me in the condo, and he went and found him another place."

"I'm still trying to figure out how you ended up sleeping with Dion." I watched her as she kept her eyes on the road.

"Hold up. This conversation is going to places it doesn't need to go."

"But, Mom, I'm just trying to understand what happened." I turned away and looked straight ahead.

"All you need to know is, I made a mistake. I slept with my friend's husband. I'm not proud of it, but it happened. The end result is, I was blessed with a daughter who I wouldn't trade for the world."

Some of the anger I felt toward my mom melted a little, and I do mean a little. "But you should have told him, and maybe we wouldn't be going through this situation now."

"You're young and wise. I wasn't thinking rational. Now I see that. Trey was willing to accept you as his own, so I didn't feel like rocking the boat. Anyway, we're at this place now, so we both need to deal with it."

We rode the rest of the way home in silence, both caught up in our own thoughts. I hightailed it to my room but stopped when I saw my dad in the hallway.

"So, how did it go?" he asked, as he followed me inside my room.

"It was easy. Dion said he's going to rush the test results."

"Really? Well, kiddo, if you want to talk, I'm here."

I threw my backpack on the bed and gave my dad a hug. "Thanks, Dad."

"Let me go find your mom. There's something I need to discuss with her."

"She's downstairs somewhere."

Once I got settled in, I texted Danielle and Tara and asked them to call me when they got a chance. Before I could hit SEND, my cell phone was ringing.

"What happened?" Danielle asked from the other end.

I told her about the test and when I should get the results. I don't know who was more nervous about my situation, she or I. "Danielle, calm down. You're making me anxious."

"All I'm saying is, Dion McNeil is your father. Now how cool is that?" she asked.

"Well, I guess it's cool, but I already have a cool dad."

"Now you'll have two."

~ 14 ~

The next day at school, I was disappointed to receive the results of several of my tests; I barely passed. It wasn't my fault that my mind hadn't been on school lately. I resigned myself to the fact that my perfect grade point average would no longer be perfect. Now, what I needed to do was maintain a B average. All that depended on what happened with Dion after he received the DNA test results. Waiting for those results had me on pins and needles. The days leading up to the DNA test results seemed to drag on.

"Porsha, are you okay?" Cole walked up to me and asked.

I was leaning on my locker and in deep thought. "Yes, I'm fine."

"I called your name out a few times, and you didn't even acknowledge me," he responded.

"Got a lot on my mind." I stood up straight.

"Do you want to talk about it?" he asked.

I could get lost in his big brown eyes. "Family stuff. I'll be all right," I responded. "You want to walk me to class?"

"Sure. So what's the latest you can receive phone calls?" he asked, as we walked down the hallway.

"Anytime. If I can't talk, I just let the phone go to voice mail."

"Cool. That's what's up. I'll be calling you tonight, if that's okay."

"I'll be looking forward to your call."

Some of the other kids seemed to be watching us. I ignored the jealous stares from some of the girls. A few turned their noses up at me as we walked by them. I loved Cole's sense of humor, so I made it a point to laugh a little louder than necessary.

We were now standing in front of my class. He surprised me when he handed me a folded up piece of paper. "Read it when you get a chance. I'll call you tonight," Cole said.

Before I could respond, he turned and walked down the hall to his class. I held on to the paper and didn't open it until I was seated behind my desk. The note read:

"I think you're the prettiest girl in the school and smart too. I really want to get to know you better. Can you come to my game Friday night? Maybe, later we can also grab something to eat."

I was so excited that I failed to acknowledge the teacher's question that was directed at me.

"Ms. Swint, see me after class, please."

"Yes, ma'am," I responded. Embarrassed, I held my head down. I wanted to slide down in my seat.

Class dragged on. I attempted to slip out without the teacher noticing, but she caught me at the door. "What's going on with you? Do you need to talk to one of the counselors?"

"No, Mrs. Jones. Just had a lot on my mind."

"Your grades are slipping. You got two zeros for not turning in your homework." She looked down at her notebook. "You'll have a chance to make it up if you do the extra project."

I wasn't too thrilled about the zero nor doing an extra project. I had more important things on my mind than school. I gave her a blank stare. "I'll try to do better," I managed to say.

She handed me two pages of stapled papers. "You have until Monday."

I took it from her and slipped it in my backpack, with no intention of doing the extra assignment. Danielle and Tara were walking past the room when I exited. "Guess what?" I ran up to them to say.

Danielle said, "We already heard—Cole walked you to class. Heard some girls talking about it."

I tilted my head back. "Really? Who? It just happened. Word travels fast."

Tara said, "Well, one of them was Jas."

"Who?" I asked.

"Jasmine. Oh my God. I just realized something. She's your half-sister. I didn't even think of that," Tara blurted.

I grabbed her by the arm to pull her to the side. "Shh. Everybody don't need to be up in my business."

"Does she know?" Danielle asked from behind me.

"I don't know." I hadn't thought about whether she knew or not. I hadn't been running into her, so it never crossed my mind to go up to her and ask her. If she knew, she could come up to me.

"I hope you don't start acting like her, with her diva-like attitude," Tara stated.

"Please. I'm better than that."

We're each near our destinations by now.

"Let me know when she knows. I'm sure she's not going to like sharing the spotlight," Danielle said, as she pulled out her lip gloss from her backpack and applied some.

"You two just love drama," I said, eyeing Danielle's tube of lip gloss, wishing I had the grape delight flavor, instead of the cherry blossom that I'd put on earlier.

"You know it," Tara responded. She and Danielle gave each other a high-five.

"Look what I got." I waved Cole's note back and forth in the air.

Tara reached for it.

I pulled it back. "I don't know if I want y'all to read it," I said, teasing them.

"Girl, you better let us see that note."

We stood near the wall as others passed us by. I watched Danielle and Tara read the note.

"I'm so happy for you," Tara said.

Danielle said, "What are we wearing?"

"We?" I asked.

"Yes. You don't think we're going to let you go to the game by yourself. Besides, Cole isn't the only one on the basketball team that has my eye," Danielle responded with a sly grin on her face.

Tara said, "You're such a hater."

"No, I'm not. I'm just saying." Danielle pouted.

I took the note and put it in a slot in my backpack. "Well, as my best friends, it is your duty to be there for me. I do expect you both to be there."

Tara said, "I can't. I'm babysitting. My mom's going out of town this weekend."

I tried not to show my disappointment. I was going to be nervous and wanted both of my besties there. "Dani, don't stand me up now."

"Oh, I will be there. I just got to figure out what I'm wearing."

"Well, I'm going to my class before I get marked tardy." I walked away and went directly to my class.

~ 15 ~

I was in a better mood when I got home from school because of anticipating Cole's phone call. I knew he had basketball practice, so when he didn't call until after nine, I wasn't surprised.

"So are you coming?" he asked in his husky voice.

"Me and my best friend Dani will be there."

"Cool. I'll give you the tickets, so you won't have to pay."

Such a gentleman, I thought. I thanked him, and we spent the rest of the time getting to know one another better. We both agreed that Drake and Nicki Minaj were our favorite rappers.

"My favorite singer is Trey Songz," I informed him.

"Yours and my baby sister's," he said.

"Well, I bet Beyoncé is yours, right?"

"Of course." He chuckled.

Cole had the cutest laugh I had ever heard. Cuter than even mine. We continued to talk about music.

"I've had my eye on you for a while," he confessed.

I was feeling all mushy inside just from the sound of his voice. "How long is a while?" I asked. I lay on my back looking at the ceiling as we talked.

"Since sophomore year."

"Really? Why haven't you said anything?" I asked.

"You had a boyfriend, and then I saw you with that dude Kenneth. Plus, believe it or not, I'm a little shy."

"What made you approach me in a crowded cafeteria, if you're so shy?"

"I lost a bet with myself, so I had to do it then, or else I never would have gotten up the nerve to."

"I won't bite you," I said, teasing him.

"I'm glad I did. You're really nice, Porsha. Nothing like some of the other girls up there."

"Thanks. Most people don't call me nice. Spoiled, maybe, but nice? I hardly ever hear that word used to describe me."

"I see how you interact with people. You seem to get along with everybody," he said.

"Almost everybody," I responded. I could name quite a few people at school who, if given the opportunity to fight me, would.

"After the game, some of us are going to Chuck's for burgers. Would you like to go?" Cole asked.

"I'm sure that won't be a problem. I just have to figure out how I'm going to get there and back."

"I have a car. I can drop you off at home."

"I need to check with my parents first, and then I'll let you know."

"I can talk to them if they want, even give them my mom's number," he responded.

"I'm sure all of that won't be necessary."

"Well, I know if you were my daughter, I would take all the precautions I could."

"So, are you saying you're a bad influence?" My voice sounded light.

"Oh, no. I might need to tell my mama where I'm at, so you won't be trying to influence me to do something I don't want to do."

We both laughed. Hanging out with Cole was going to be a blast. I glanced at the clock. "Oh my goodness. It's almost twelve o'clock. I better get off here. I already dread getting up in the morning."

"I'll see you at school. Good night, Porsha . . . my future girlfriend."

"You got a lot of confidence, mister star basketball player."

"And you know it. Good night," he said.

"Good night." I held the phone in my hand for a few seconds before placing it on the nightstand near my bed.

I slid under the covers and each time I closed my eyes I thought of Cole. I replayed our conversations in my head. I could feel myself blush when I thought about him calling me his future girlfriend. His beautiful smile brightened my dream world. I woke up the next morning with a smile on my face.

It was now two more days left before the DNA test results. Tension in the kitchen was thicker than a brick. My parents snapped at each other. "We can talk later," my mom said to my dad.

I could tell my mom had been crying because of her puffy eyes. I was sure the issue was Dion. I felt sad for my dad because of what he was going through. On the other hand, it was hard to feel sympathy for my mom. Don't get me wrong. I was no longer mad at her like I was when I'd first found out about this messed up situation. But she still wasn't one hundred percent back in good standing with me.

"Dear, your dad is dropping you off at school today. I have to be at the boys' school this morning," she said.

I shrugged my shoulders, grabbed a blueberry muffin off the table and took a bite out of it. "I'm ready."

My dad grunted, threw the newspaper he had been reading on the table and said, "Let's go."

My mom's eyes pled with me to say something else, but I didn't give her the satisfaction. I followed my dad out of the kitchen and to his SUV.

Once safely on the highway, he addressed me. "You shouldn't be so hard on her. She's really sorry for what happened."

"I'm sorry too."

"What's going on with you? Yesterday, you seemed fine. This morning, not so much."

I was fine until I saw their sour faces. *Should I or shouldn't I tell him the truth?* I opted to say, "Just one of those days."

He laughed, but not one of those funny laughs. One of those "you-got-to-be-kidding—me" type laughs. "You haven't seen anything yet. Wait until you become an adult. You'll see a lot of those days."

I hoped not. Dealing with what I was dealing with now was enough to last me a lifetime.

"Baby girl, this is an adjustment for us all. I want this transition to happen as smooth as possible, but with life comes bumps, and this is one of them."

"I know, but why now? I just wished things could go back to how they used to be," I said.

"Me too, but it can't, so all we can do is deal with it. Deal with it together. Because one thing hasn't changed, and you know what that is?"

I shook my head. "No."

"We're a family. Family gets through things together. When it's all said and done, we still have each other."

The talk we had on the way to school made me feel much better.

~ 16 ~

"Did you ask your folks about your party?" Tara asked, as we sat across from each other at lunch.

Oops. I had totally forgotten about my sweet sixteen party. "No, I haven't. I got so much other stuff on my mind."

"Like Cole," Danielle teased.

"Hating is not a pretty color on you," I responded.

"Here he comes now," Tara said.

I looked up at Cole, who was headed straight for our table, along with one of his teammates.

"Do you mind if we sit with y'all?"

"No. Let me move over," Danielle said, as she batted her eyes.

I rolled my eyes. I scooted my chair over to give them more space.

Cole placed his tray near me. "This is my boy Rob," he said.

I made the other introduction. "This is Danielle and Tara."

After exchanging pleasantries, we all went to eating our food.

Cole reached into his pocket and handed me something. "I only got you two tickets, but if you need a third one, I can get you one."

Tara said, "I can't go. Maybe I can catch one of your games another time."

"Hopefully so, because I'm a beast on the court," Rob said, although Tara was talking to Cole and not him.

Danielle remained awfully quiet. Normally, she would be trying to take over the conversation. She seemed to be upset that Rob was paying Tara more attention than her.

Cole and I blocked out the three of them and got into our personal conversation.

"I really want you to consider being my girl," he said.

"But we haven't known each other long." I attempted to remind him.

"We've been at the same school for years. Don't pretend like you didn't know who I was." He stuck out his chest.

Cole was correct. I knew exactly who he was. He was not only the cute guy, but he was smart. His grades were just as good as mine, well, as good as they were, because I had let them slip a little lately. Flirting with Cole was fun. It also kept my mind off the problems I had at home.

"So, are you going to be mine?"

"Maybe. I'll let you know," I responded. I tilted my head back a little.

"You're so cute when you do that," he said.

I blushed. "You're cute when you say things like that."

"Oh my goodness, you two need to quit," Rob said.

"Man, stop hating. Get your own girl," Cole turned his face around and said. "Now, what was I saying?"

"You were telling me how pretty I am," I responded.

"That you are."

"Pretty girls rock," Danielle added.

I guess she was tired of not being part of anyone's conversation, so she was sticking her two cents into mine.

From that moment on, we all made small talk. Cole and I stole hidden glances at each other. I didn't know why I was fronting because I wanted to be Cole's girl, and although things were moving a little fast, after the game on Friday, I was going to give him an answer.

Cole walked me to my class after lunch. When we reached near the door, he gave me a quick hug. It was so quick, I almost missed it. "See you later," he said, before bouncing down the hall.

"No physical touching, young lady," Mr. Trudeau said, as I passed him in the doorway.

I slipped in my seat behind my desk with my head down, hoping none of the other students had heard him. I barely passed the pop quiz he gave us. My concentration level was nil. I could have stayed home for what good I was doing at school.

In between classes, I checked my cell phone. Cole's text message said, "Thinking of you. Call you tonight."

True to his word, later on that night, Cole called. "I aced Mr. Trudeau's test," he bragged.

Ashamed that I didn't, I hoped he didn't ask me how I did. To my relief, he didn't. "Rumor has it that some of the NBA scouts are looking at you. Is that true?" I asked.

"Not sure. I just play the best game I can every time I'm on the court."

"Cool. You're good. My dad thinks you're one of the best players he's seen in a while," I said.

"Really? I went to a summer camp when I was nine, and your dad inspired me to not only give my all to being a good basketball player, but he's the reason why I make sure I keep my grades up too."

Wow! I was impressed and proud of my dad. "He's a cool dad."

"I have his autographed jersey in a case hanging on my wall."

Uh-oh. I hope Cole wasn't only interested in me because of Trey Swint, the former all-star running back of the NFL. If so, our relationship would be over before it even got started. I listened to him go on and on about my dad for as long as I could before I interrupted him. "I don't know how to say this, so I'm just going to come out and say it. Cole, I'm tired of talking about my dad."

"Porsha, I'm sorry. When it comes to sports, I can get a little carried away."

"I'm going to be honest with you. I'm sort of wondering if you want to talk to me because of who my dad is, or if you really want to be with me, Porsha."

"You can get that idea out of your head. I can have any girl I want, but I want you. You could act like a spoiled brat, but you don't. I like you, Ms. Porsha Swint, for the sweet person on the inside."

I didn't know if I should believe him, but he was pouring the syrup on thick, and I was eating it up. I smiled like I was auditioning for a toothpaste commercial. "I wanted to make sure because, if that's the case, then I would have to kick you to the curb."

"So, does that mean you'll be my girl?"

"I'll let you know after the game."

"Can't wait to game time then," Cole said.

~ 17 ~

Cole and I were dancing to our own little tune as we talked to way past midnight. That night I fell asleep with a smile on my face but woke up groggy from lack of sleep.

"Porsha, wake up," my mom said, as she shook me a few times.

"What time is it?" I asked, as I tried to retreat back under the covers.

My mom wasn't having it. She pulled the covers back. "If you stayed off the phone at night, you could get up."

Busted. How did she know? "I'm getting up, okay."

"Now. I have a lot of errands to run this morning."

"Can't Dad take me?" I asked.

"No. Now get your behind out of that bed, Porsha Marie."

I knew I was in trouble when my mama called me by my first and middle name. I got up and got dressed in less than thirty minutes.

She was waiting for me near the front door when I made it downstairs. "Grab you a muffin because we don't have time for you to eat cereal," she said.

I obeyed and then met her at the car. "Mom, I've been meaning to ask if I could have a sweet sixteen party."

"Dear, maybe we should table this for later."

"But it's not my fault all of this mess is going on." The rage inside of me was threatening to rear its ugly head.

"Fine. You can have your party. We got you so spoiled," she snapped.

Right now my mom was like the "wicked witch of the south." She should have been doing anything she could to make me happy, but no. She wanted to give me major attitude. It's not my fault we were in this situation. It was all hers. I crossed my arms, leaned back in the seat and looked out the passenger window. I had another question to ask her, but didn't want to. But I had to, so my friends and I could make our plans.

"How many people can I invite, and can I have a theme?" I asked.

"Look, I wasn't going to tell you this, but since you keep asking all of these questions, your dad and I have already planned your sweet sixteen party."

A smile swept across my face. "Really, Mom? Why didn't y'all tell me?" I forgot all about being mad at her.

"It was supposed to be a surprise. But I just hadn't had a chance to contact Danielle or Tara."

"Well, they've been bugging me about it because I'm the first out of all of us to turn sixteen."

"You can invite one hundred people. No more, you understand me. And Danielle and Tara are included in that hundred."

"Yes, ma'am."

"One other thing, just because we're giving you your dream party, don't think it means you're not still responsible for cleaning your room and other chores."

"You're the greatest, Mom."

"Yeah, right."

I could see a smile forming on her face.

"Oh, no need to pick me up today. Danielle and I are going to the basketball game today after school."

"And when were you going to tell me?"

"Like you said, with everything going on, I forgot." I pouted. For a moment, I thought she was going to tell me I couldn't go.

Instead she said, "You know today's the day Dion gets the DNA tests back."

How could I forget? "Yes. But that shouldn't change whether or not I can go to the game."

"Go to the game. What time is it over, so your dad or I will be sure to come by to pick you up?"

"Danielle's cousin is picking us up," I lied.

"Which one of her cousins?" my mom asked.

"I forget her name." My eyes darted away. Since my mom was driving, she couldn't look into my eyes to tell I was lying.

"Just be home no later than ten o'clock, since it's a Friday."

"But what about food? I know I'm going to be hungry. Can I get an extra hour so we can swing by and get us something to eat?" I pled.

"Eleven o'clock. Not one minute after."

"Thanks, Mom," I said, as she pulled up in front of my school. I now didn't feel guilty about the change of clothes I had in my book bag that I hadn't told my mom about. I knew she didn't think I was going to wear this uniform to the game.

I sent a text to Danielle and Tara while I was walking up the walkway to inform them of the party and the game. "Excuse me," a screechy voice said, as I accidentally bumped into someone.

My eyes were more on my phone than what was ahead, so I was in the wrong. I looked up, and it was Jasmine. "I'm sorry," I said.

"Next time watch where you're going," she snapped.

"I said I was sorry. Dang!"

"Whatever." Jasmine rolled her eyes and then stormed in the opposite direction.

I heard Jasmine's friend Britney say, "Jasmine, she didn't try to," as she followed behind her.

A part of me hoped the DNA test results came back and said Dion was not my biological father, because having Jasmine as a sister was bound to be a pain.

Anyhow, my BFFs both responded that they would bring their list of names to the cafeteria at lunch so we could finalize my guest list.

The first part of my day seemed to drag on. My mom texted me to call her, so in between classes, I slipped into the girls' restroom and called her.

"The tests results are back, baby."

I inhaled and held my breath.

"Dion now knows for sure that without a doubt you're his daughter," my mom continued to say. "Dear, are you there?"

I exhaled. "Yes, Mom. Thanks for letting me know."

It was now official. I was Dion McNeil's daughter. No more pretending. Going to Cole's basketball game didn't have the same appeal anymore.

"Mom, I might have you come pick me up after school. I'm not sure about going to the game anymore."

I got off the phone and went into one of the bathroom stalls and cried.

~ 18 ~

"Porsha, you have to go. What about Cole? You told him you would be there. Plus, I bought this new outfit. Girl, come on. Please don't bail out on me," Danielle pled with me after I told her and Tara during lunch that I wasn't feeling the game anymore.

Tara agreed with Danielle. "You knew the results were coming back today. It's not like it was a big surprise anyway. Your mom said he was your dad. That was something he was doing for himself. It shouldn't stop you from having fun."

I thought about what they were saying. They were right. I sent my mom a quick text to let her know that I was still going to the game. She sent me a smiley face response back.

Danielle said, "Now that it's settled, let's get to your guest list. Here's my list." She handed me a sheet of paper filled with names.

I scanned the paper. "Uh, I don't think so. She doesn't even speak to me." I used my pen and scratched a line through the name. I ended up scratching out half the people on her list for one reason or another. "Tara, let me see yours."

"I don't have as many people on mine as Danielle's," Tara said, as she handed me her sheet of paper.

"Who is Cecilia?" I asked.

Tara responded, "That's the girl in my calculus class."

"I don't know her, so she goes off the list too."

Danielle gave Tara a smug look. "Now you see how it feels."

I laughed when Tara stuck her tongue out at Danielle. I loved my two BFFs, although they could act silly sometimes.

Cole sent me a text message to let me know he was practicing and would see me at the game. I smiled for the first time since learning that, without a doubt, Dion was my father. It was hard concentrating in my classes. One minute I was thinking about Cole, and the next minute I was thinking about what was going to happen next now that Dion knew for sure I was his. So many questions and doubts filled my mind.

Danielle and I used the gym's dressing room to change into our other clothes. We were both looking fly in our skinny jeans and colorful shirts.

"I think you should wear some red lipstick with a clear gloss over it," Danielle said, as she took out her makeup bag and made up my face.

"Make it look natural now. I don't want it to look like I'm getting all pretty just for him," I said.

"Please. You better try to look good for him. It's a lot of girls that will be there trying to get his attention."

"Dani, thanks. Now I'm going to be self-conscious."

"I just want you to be on top of your game. Let them chicks know you got it like that and they better step back because Cole is yours."

From out of nowhere, Jasmine appeared. "He's not yours yet. So, if I were you, I would wipe that off your face and start over."

Before I could say anything, Danielle responded, "No one was talking to you. This is an A and B conversation, so please *see* your way out of it."

"I just don't want your girl to get disappointed. You know, we sisters have to stick together." With that snide remark, Jasmine left the dressing room.

"Does she know?" Danielle asked.

I shrugged my shoulders up and down. "I have no idea. I'm sure she'll find out soon, if she doesn't."

"I would watch my back. Sounds like she has her eyes set on your man."

"It's up to Cole. I'm not fighting over a guy."

"Wimp. You give up too easily," Danielle said, as she went to making up her face.

"I'm just saying . . . I don't fight over guys. If a guy is interested in me, then he will not be all up in some other girl's face."

"Like your boy Kenneth," Danielle added.

"Don't remind me. I don't even see what I saw in him." I cringed at the thought of Kenneth at this point.

"Ladies, I'm about to close up this area, so hurry up," one of the female janitors said.

"We're almost through," I responded.

A few minutes later, Danielle and I were headed to the gym, where the game was being held. We handed the attendant our tickets and went to our floorside seat. I noticed Jasmine and her friends in the bleachers. I switched my hips as I passed by some of the team working out. Cole caught my eye and waved at me. I waved back. I looked in the direction of Jasmine, and I could feel the venom seeping through her eyes. I smiled and winked at her and sashayed to my seat.

Cole slipped up next to us and said, "Glad you came. See you after the game." Before you know it, he was back down the court with his other team members.

Yes, Jasmine and the rest of y'all girls who want my man, eat your hearts out, because Cole is mine.

Danielle and I cheered along with the crowd as our home team outscored the visitors by a few points. The last few minutes of the game, the scores were tied. I scooted to the edge of my seat as the score kept going back and forth. With only a few seconds left on the clock, I held my breath when the ball was thrown to Cole. I glanced at the scoreboard clock. With less than ten seconds and a half court away, he bounced the ball, and within seconds the ball was in the air. The buzzer ending the game sounded as the net swooshed and the ball entered through the rim. The crowd jumped up for joy as Cole's shot gave Plano High a victory.

Danielle and I jumped up and hugged each other. "We won! We won!" Danielle yelled.

People from the stands chanted Cole's name. I beamed with pride as his teammates and others congratulated him. Danielle and I waited in the stands as the crowd dispersed. My cell phone vibrated. I glanced at it. "Dani, Cole wants us to meet him out front."

"I hope he brings one of his cute friends with him."

"I'm sure he will. He wants all of my attention, and he won't be able to do it with you in my ear."

~ 19 ~

Cole invited his teammate Eric Boyd along with him, and he and Danielle seemed to get along great. When we walked into Chuck's Burgers, people stopped and cheered for Cole and the rest of his teammates. Cole placed his arm around me and led us to a table near the back. I couldn't help but notice the jealous stares from some of the girls in the place.

A waitress brought over two sodas and placed one in front of Cole and one in front of Eric. She said, "These are from the girls at that table."

All four sets of eyes turned toward the table. *Trashy* was the only word I could think of. Those girls knew Cole and Eric were with us.

To my surprise, Cole said, "You can take the drinks back to their table. I can buy my own drinks."

Yes, I screamed inside, a huge smile covering my face.

Cole and I talked in between his teammates stopping by his table. He introduced me as his girl, and I beamed with pride. Afterward we dropped Danielle and Eric off at home. I didn't live that far from Danielle, so Cole took his time driving on the side streets.

"Finally, I have you to myself," he said, as he reached across the seat for my hand.

My heart rate increased as his hand held mine. "I had a great time tonight," I said.

"Next time, it'll just be me and you," he assured me.

By now, we were pulling up near my house. "I only have ten minutes left before my curfew," I said.

Cole turned and looked in my direction. The light from the moon beaming allowed our eyes to focus on one another. "Porsha, I've waited all night to ask you this. Will you be my girl?"

Without hesitating, I responded, "Yes."

He removed his seatbelt, moved across the seat and, as if in slow motion, I watched as his lips came toward me. No, this wasn't my first time being kissed by a boy, but it sure felt like it. When his lips touched mine, time stood still. His soft lips covered mine. I wondered if he could hear my rapid heartbeat.

Although the kiss took only a few seconds, it left a lasting impression on me. I had to get out of the car and fast. "Cole, I don't want to be late, because my mom will kill me."

"Let me walk you to the door," he said as he shifted back in his seat.

"No," I blurted. "I'll wave to you when I get in the house."

"You sure?" he said.

I reached over the seat and gave him a quick peck. "Good night, Cole."

Cole waited until he saw me enter the house. I turned around and waved. He blinked the car lights. He didn't pull off until after I closed the door. I peeped out the window and watched him pull away.

"Did you have a nice time?" my mom asked, startling me.

I wondered if she saw me and Cole in the car. "Yes, ma'am."

"Good. Well, get you some sleep. We'll talk in the morning."

I avoided eye contact with my mom and went straight to the bathroom. I took a quick shower and then got ready for bed. I noticed I had a few missed calls from Cole. I made sure my door was closed and then slipped in bed and returned his call.

"You've made me the happiest boy at Plano High," he said, as he thanked me for agreeing to be his girl.

"I'm pretty lucky myself," I responded, blushing, as I slipped under the covers.

"We get senior rings next week. I want you to wear mine," he said.

"Really? Wow!" Things were moving fast. Cole was smart, he was cute, and he was the star basketball player. What more could a girl like me want?

When my eyes closed that night, my thoughts were on Cole and the fact that I had a new boyfriend. One I absolutely adored, and who seemed to adore me too. At least one thing was going right in my life. Tomorrow would bring its own set of problems, but for the night I would concentrate on the joys of being Cole's girl.

My vibrating phone woke me up out of my sound sleep the next morning. "Hello," I said sluggishly.

Cole's voice was on the other end. "I can't get you off my mind. I had to hear your voice before I left for practice."

Aw, how sweet, I thought. "What time is it?" I asked.

"It's almost ten."

"Really? I guess I need to get up and start my day," I responded, although I had no immediate plans.

"I'll call you later," he said.

Once our call ended, I sat up in bed. I stared off and recalled what happened when he dropped me off at home. I was still in that love zone when my mom entered my room, without knocking, mind you.

"Dear, you can't stay in the bed all day. Dion is coming over later to talk to me and your dad. I just wanted you to know. He'll be here around three."

"Did he say anything about seeing me?" I asked, forgetting Cole for a moment.

"I'm sure he'll want to see you."

I pouted. What if he didn't? I didn't even want to find out. "I'm getting dressed now," I said, slipping off from underneath the covers.

"By the way, I saw the young man who brought you home. Next time, introduce us, otherwise, you won't be going to any more games."

Busted. "He's Cole. He's our star basketball player."

"Star or not, you know how I feel about boys."

"But you said I could date. Are you backing off that now?" I blurted out.

"We have no problems with you dating, but we need to know the boy and something about his family."

"He's Cole, Mom. He's a nice guy. He gets good grades. Ask Dad. He knows about him," I said in Cole's defense.

~ 20 ~

Thirty minutes later, my dad was interrogating me about Cole. "Your mom told me you're dating again."

I went on to tell him about Cole. "I thought you liked him."

"He's a good ballplayer, but I don't know enough about him to say I want him dating my daughter."

"He's a good guy, Dad."

"So when do we get to meet this young man?"

"I can call him, and he can come over today."

"Today's not a good day. Dealing with Dion later is all the excitement your old man can take in one day."

"Pick a date, and I'm sure he'll be thrilled to meet you." I went on to tell my dad about his autographed jersey Cole had adorning his wall.

"The young man has good taste, but still I need to check him out." He hugged me and then left me alone with my thoughts.

I sent Cole a short text informing him that my parents wanted to meet him. He was excited. Normally guys dreaded meeting my parents. *Maybe we could make it happen next weekend,* I thought.

After going back and forth via text with Cole, I got online and surfed the entertainment gossip sites. I also chatted with Danielle and Tara in our own private chat room. They sent me congratulatory messages when I informed them of my new girlfriend title. I stuck my chest out with pride knowing my friends approved of my decision.

Time seemed to drag on as I kept watching the clock hoping that three o'clock would hurry up and come so I could see if Dion wanted to see me.

The doorbell rang, and I rushed to my window to see who was outside. I noticed Dion's car parked in the driveway. I gave myself a quick glance in the mirror. It seemed like I was holding my breath when my mom shouted, "Porsha, can you come here?"

The steps I took to reach downstairs doubled as each step took me closer to a new destiny. There, standing at the end of the stairway, was Dion. His reassuring smile eased some of my fears.

"Porsha, it's good seeing you again," he said.

"Hi," was the only word I managed to say.

My dad said, "Angie's fixed dinner, so let's go to the dining room."

Everyone was polite over dinner. Dion and my dad talked about sports, while my mom and I seemed to be on edge.

"Porsha, how's school?" Dion asked.

"Everything's fine." Even if it wasn't, I didn't feel comfortable sharing that news with him just yet.

"Porsha's a straight-A student," my dad said with pride.

If only he knew my grades had slipped. My A was slowly fading to a borderline B, and only points away from a C. "I do all right." I wouldn't look in anyone's eyes.

"She's also active in many school organizations," my mom added.

What were they doing? It's as if I was in an interview for a job or something. They both needed to quit.

I was glad my two little brothers were gone. It made me wonder when my folks were going to reveal to them about my real dad. Or were we supposed to keep it a secret from them?

My mom went and brought out dessert. One of my favorites, strawberry shortcake.

"Dion, I have a question."

We all looked in Mom's direction.

She asked, "Do your other kids know about Porsha?"

My head swung in his direction. He cleared his throat. "No, not yet."

"So when do you plan on breaking the news to them? Because my child will not be your little secret."

"I plan on telling them tomorrow. In fact, Porsha, I would love it if you could come over tomorrow, so I can make the introductions."

"This is all moving so fast," I blurted out without thinking.

"I want us to build a relationship. I want you to know your sisters," he responded.

My dad said, "Give her some time. Maybe, next weekend."

Dion said, "They go to the same school. I think it's best that I make the introductions face to face."

My mom agreed. "Dear, Dion might be right. We will bring her," she said, emphasizing the word *we*.

My dad clenched his fist. I wasn't sure if anyone else noticed, but I did. "Fine. What time?"

"Around the same time. I'll throw some food on the grill."

After dinner, my dad rushed Dion out the door. "We have to go pick up our sons, but we'll see you tomorrow."

"Okay. Sounds good. Oh, before I forget, Porsha, here's all my numbers." Dion reached into his wallet and passed me a card.

I looked at it before my hand fell to the side.

We all stood there and watched him get in his car. Once the door was closed, my mom said, "See, that wasn't too bad, now was it?"

"Did you have to side with him?" my dad asked in a harsh tone.

"Dear, I wasn't siding with him. Porsha needs to meet her sisters, so why not tomorrow?"

"This is what I was worried about. Already, you're blocking me out of the decision-making," he said and stormed out of the house.

"Trey," my mom called out in vain.

He threw his arms up in the air and jumped in his SUV and pulled away.

My mom started sobbing.

I placed my arm around her. "Dad just needs time to cool down. It'll be okay."

"Things will never be okay again," she said, as she sobbed in my arms.

Why am I comforting her and I'm the one with a new daddy? Stranger things had happened, and we held on to each other for dear life.

~ 21 ~

I knew something wasn't right when my mom allowed me to sleep past nine on a Sunday morning. Once again, we were missing Sunday church services. I thought now was the time for us to draw closer to the Lord, not pull further away. I said a silent prayer before starting my day.

I knocked on my parents' door.

"Come in," my dad said.

When I entered, he was sitting on the edge of the bed with his pajamas on.

Mom was sitting on her side of the bed, covered up by her robe. Her eyes looked swollen. "Can you fix Jay and Jason some breakfast, dear?" she asked.

"Sure. Everything all right in here?" I asked.

"Yes," they both snapped.

I knew they both were lying. I eased out of their room.

Jay and Jason were busy downstairs playing their video game. "Y'all need to go wash your funky behinds," I yelled.

"You're the one stanking," Jason responded.

"I can smell your breath all the way over here," Jay added.

They laughed, but I didn't.

"I'm about to cook breakfast, and if you want to eat, you better get your baths."

"You're not our mama," Jay said.

"But I'm your older sister, so you better do what I say."

"Make us," Jason said, holding the remote with both of his hands.

"Fine. Don't do what I say. When I tell Dad you disobeyed me, then you'll have him to deal with." I crossed my arms in front of me.

"We were just playing," Jason said, a sly grin on his face.

Jay added, "You need to lighten up. Can't you take a joke?"

"Whatever. You two brats get on my nerves." I stormed out of the room to the kitchen.

Thirty minutes later, I had breakfast fixed. Jason and Jay were dressed in jeans and T-shirts and gobbled down the turkey bacon, eggs, and grits I cooked.

"These biscuits are hard," Jason commented.

"No, they're not. Now eat it."

Jason threw the biscuit at Jay.

"Ouch!" Jay yelled.

"See? Told you they were hard." Jason laughed.

"Good to see some things haven't changed," Dad said, as he entered the kitchen.

"Dad, I made enough for you and Mom too. Want me to get it for you?" I asked.

"No, baby girl. I'll get it. You all just finish eating," he responded.

Once seated, he addressed the boys. "I need to talk to you about something as soon as I finish eating, so don't go outside."

"But, Dad, it's a pretty day for us to go bike riding," Jason said.

"You heard what I said."

"Yes, sir," Jason said, as he hung his head down.

"You too, dear, don't go anywhere. We're having a family meeting."

My mom never came down to eat, but she did meet us in the living room for our family meeting. She wore shades to cover up her puffy eyes. I looked at her and then back at my dad. Jason and Jay were wrestling.

She snapped, "Stop that, boys. What we have to talk about is serious."

They stopped doing what they were doing.

My dad said, "Everybody listen up. The dynamics of our life is about to change."

Now, I knew what he wanted to talk about. I wondered how it would affect my relationship with my brothers. I listened as my dad went on to say, "You all know that we love you, right?"

Jason, Jay, and I nodded our heads up and down in agreement.

Mom said, "I hope this will only bring our family closer."

"Are you dying, Mom?" Jason blurted.

"No, dear, I'm in good health, as far as I know."

"Well, what is it?" Jay asked.

My dad sat down near my mom. He sighed. "Porsha is your sister, but I'm not her father," he said, his voice sounding pained.

"I don't understand," Jay said.

Jason informed him. "Porsha has another baby daddy."

Since my parents seemed to have a hard time explaining things, I decided to take over. "What Dad is saying is, he's not my blood father."

"So you're not our sister. That means I don't have to do anything you tell me to do," Jay responded.

"I'll always be your sister. We share the same mom. We just have two different fathers. Like your friends Mike and Gerald."

"Oh, yeah. Well, who's your real dad then?" Jason asked.

"Dion McNeil," I responded.

"*The* Dion McNeil?" Jay and Jason passed looks with one another.

"The one and same," I responded.

"Cool. Well, it is cool, isn't it?" Jay asked, as he looked directly at my parents.

"Yes, it's a cool thing that Porsha has two men she can call daddy," my mom said, removing the sunglasses and revealing her puffy eyes.

"So when do we get to meet him?" Jay asked.

"I want his autograph, so my friends at school can be jealous," Jason added.

"Well, we really don't know. Later on today, I will be taking Porsha to spend time with her father," my mom said.

"While the three of us go to the park and hang out," Dad added.

It appeared that Jason and Jay were the only two excited about Dion McNeil being my biological father. The rest of us were just going along with the emotions until we knew what would happen next.

~ 22 ~

"Where are you going with that on?" my mom asked.

"We're going to a cookout. How else was I supposed to dress?" I responded. I had on my skinny jeans and a blue Dallas Cowboys jersey.

She ignored me and went to my walk-in closet. She walked back out with a pink and yellow knee-length design springtime dress and matching sandals. "Put this on."

"But, Mom . . . "

"But Mom, nothing. This is the first time meeting your sisters, and I want you to look nice."

"There isn't anything wrong with this."

"Change! You got ten minutes."

Without another word, my mom left, and reluctantly I did as I was told. I had to admit, after changing I did look nicer. I ran into my dad out in the hallway.

"Don't you look cute," he commented.

I blushed. "Thanks, Dad."

"Now, if you need me, call me," he said, as we walked downstairs.

My dad surprised me when he gave my mom a kiss on the lips before we left the house. I guess they had made up. Yes, indeed. The smile on her face confirmed it.

"Put your seatbelt on," she said, while backing out of the driveway.

We didn't have to drive too far to reach Dion's house. Our house was a nice size, but Dion's seemed more extravagant. There were several cars outside when we arrived.

"Don't be nervous," my mom said, more to herself than to me.

We both checked our reflections in the mirror. I retraced my lips with a tube of watermelon lip gloss, smacked them together, and exited the car with my mom.

"Let me do the talking at first, okay," she said.

"Sure." She didn't have to worry. I wasn't going to say anything, unless spoken to.

The walk up the sidewalk leading to the front door seemed to take us forever. I pushed the doorbell, and a woman dressed in an apron opened. "Come on in. You must be Porsha and Porsha's mom," the woman said.

"Yes. I'm Angela."

We shook her hand.

"Well, Dion is expecting you. Everyone's outside on the patio."

"Nice," my mom said, as we followed the woman toward the patio.

I stood at the patio door for a few seconds before following behind them. Dion was grilling. Jasmine was laid out on a lawn chair talking on her phone. An older woman and a younger woman, who I recognized from their reality show, were also seated.

"Your guests are here," the woman announced.

"Betty, thank you," Dion responded.

"You two make yourselves at home. I'm going to finish making the salad so you all can eat."

My mom looked at me and gave me a reassuring smile. "Come on, dear."

I walked side by side with her, closer to where everybody sat.

Kimberly's mouth hung open. "Is this who I think it is?" she asked Dion.

"Angela, thank you for coming. Porsha, you look lovely," he said, as he walked over and greeted us.

"Hi, Kimberly," my mom said, as she sat in a chair across from hers.

"It's been, what, fifteen years?" Kimberly said.

"More like sixteen," my mom responded.

"So, are you and Dion trying to rekindle an old flame? Is that why he asked us over here?"

My mom laughed. "Please. I'm a happily married woman. Remember Trey Swint? Well, we're still together."

"Oh yeah, that's right. I think I read somewhere you two were still married." Kimberly placed her shades on her eyes and leaned back in her chair.

"Happily, I might add," my mom said.

"Oh, you don't have to convince me. You're the one here trying to seduce my husband. Correction, I mean, *ex*-husband."

"Ladies," Dion interrupted, "why don't everybody fix a plate, and then we can talk."

"I need to use the rest room," I said.

"Jas, show Porsha where the bathroom is," Dion stated.

"It's through the door and down the hallway," Jasmine yelled out.

"I said, 'show her,'" he responded, waving the spatula in his hand.

Brenda, my elder half-sister, interjected, "I'll show her."

I followed Brenda into the house. She didn't say much, but she wasn't rude to me either.

"You have to excuse Jasmine," she said. "She can sometimes act like a spoiled brat."

Brenda was gone when I got out of the bathroom. As I returned toward the patio door, a portrait of Dion, Jasmine, and Brenda in the hallway caught my attention. It appeared to be hand-painted. I reached out to touch it but pulled back.

A lone tear threatened to slide down my face. I sniffled for a few seconds, pulled myself together, and went back out to the patio to meet everyone else.

My mom had fixed me a plate. I took a seat next to her. I didn't like the looks Jasmine or her mom gave us, so I kept my attention more on the food than the company.

"So how old is your daughter?" Kimberly asked.

"Porsha will be sixteen next month," my mom responded.

"So you and Jasmine are around the same age. Jasmine will be sixteen this year too," Kimberly said.

"And I'm going to have the best sweet sixteen party Dallas has ever seen," Jasmine said.

"Well, we're throwing Porsha a party next month, so Jasmine you'll be getting an invitation soon," my mom stated.

"We're not friends."

Dion took that opportunity to interrupt. "Thank you all for coming," he said. "I didn't know how I was going to do this, but first I want everyone to hear me out, before saying anything."

Kimberly pushed her plate away from her and gave him her undivided attention. The only sounds heard were the birds chirping and dogs barking in the background.

"I'm glad my family is here today," Dion said.

"Then what is she"—Kimberly pointed at my mom—"doing here?"

My mom rolled her eyes.

"Yeah, why are they here?" Jasmine asked.

Brenda snapped at Jasmine. "If you shut up, maybe we'll find out."

Dion looked at Brenda and Jasmine. "I recently found out that Porsha is my—"

Before he could get it out, Kimberly had jumped up out of her seat and was trying to reach for my mother. "I knew you were no good," she yelled out, as her hair swung all out over the place.

~ 23 ~

I blinked my eyes and realized that what I was seeing was only a figment of my imagination. Kimberly was still sitting in her spot, and Mom was still sitting in her spot.

Dion continued his statement. " . . . daughter."

"What?" Jasmine yelled. "How is she your daughter? We're the same age."

Brenda said, "Apparently, he had an affair on Mom. Duh!"

"With that wench right there?" Kimberly was now seated on the edge of her seat, her elbows on the table.

Dion said, "Ladies, I didn't ask Angie and Porsha over here for a fight. I want my daughters to get to know each other."

Kimberly said, "Angie, you were supposed to be my friend, and this is how you betray me."

My mom responded, "We haven't been friends in sixteen years."

Kimberly squinted her eyes. "Why now? Trey running out of money and you want some of Dion's?"

Brenda asked, "Yes, why now? Why didn't you say something to us before now?"

Dion intervened. "If everyone will calm down, I'm sure Angie will be happy to answer your questions." He looked at my mom.

My mom closed her eyes, took a deep breath, and then opened her eyes and said, "Dion and I slipped up one time and made a beautiful daughter. Kim, I apologized to you then, and I'm apologizing to you now. What happened between Dion and I was a mistake, and I'm sorry."

"You can keep your sorry. I can't believe this."

My mom calmly said, "Believe it. Whether you want to accept it or not, Porsha is Dion's child and your children's sister."

Jasmine jumped up from her seat. "She is not my sister."

"Jasmine, sit down," Dion said.

Kimberly stood up too. "You will not talk to my daughter in that tone. Jasmine, get your things. We are out of here."

Jasmine grabbed her phone and e-book reader and rushed into Dion's house.

"But, Kim, I need to talk to Jasmine," Dion pled.

"You should have told her in private. You know how sensitive Jasmine is, and now she finds out you have a bastard child. Dion, hurting me was one thing, but you've hurt my child."

"Kim, wait."

Kim threw up her middle finger as my mom and I watched the whole scenario.

Brenda said, "I'll talk to them." She turned and looked in my direction. "Welcome to our crazy family."

"Glad my child didn't have to grow up with your lunatic ex-wife," Mom commented.

"Angie, don't start."

"I'm just saying." My mom chewed on her celery stick.

"None of this would have happened, if you were honest with me from the start," he responded.

My mom threw the celery stick down on her plate. "Oh, no, don't even try to put the blame on me. It takes two people to make a baby, and if memory serves me correctly, you were the one who came on to me first."

Kimberly walked from behind. "I knew it. I'm so glad I don't have to deal with you anymore." She grabbed the car keys she had left on the table and jetted back toward the house.

Dion and my mom had apparently forgotten I was sitting there as they rehashed their affair.

"You should have told me Kim was going to be here, because we wouldn't have come."

"I thought it was best. Just in case Jasmine reacted the way she just did."

"Well, anyway, it's like this. You say you want a relationship with your daughter, but I do not want her around Kim, until she can keep herself calm."

"Let me worry about Kim. Porsha, I hate you had to see that."

Now, they remember I'm here. "I knew she was a drama queen, from watching your reality show," I responded.

"Well, I don't like drama," he said.

My mom responded, "I can't tell."

"Angie, do you mind if I spend a little time alone with my daughter?"

My mom looked at me and then back at Dion. "This is something we hadn't talked about. I'm not sure about leaving her alone."

"You don't have to go anywhere. Have Betty show you where everything is. Just go inside and relax. We'll be right here."

"Porsha, are you okay with this?" Mom asked.

"I guess."

"I'll be inside." She held up her purse. "My cell's right here if you need me."

"We'll be fine, Mom," I assured her.

This was our first time alone since the test results. An awkward silence hung between us.

"Sorry about Jasmine. She can be a little dramatic at times," he said, once he did start back talking.

"She's a drama queen. I've known it since freshman year." I shrugged my shoulders.

"I meant what I said earlier. I really want us to develop a relationship."

What did he expect me to say? Did he want a medal? Instead I responded, "Oh, okay."

"I want you to know, if I knew you existed before now, I never would have disowned you."

"It's easy to say that now." I looked him straight in the eyes.

"I've never been one to back down from my responsibility."

"Well, that's good to know."

"You and Jasmine are more alike than you think. You both have a stubborn streak in you."

"I wonder where we get that from." I leaned back in my chair.

"Your mamas."

We both burst out laughing.

"My mom said you seduced her. So, is that true?" I asked.

"Probably. Back then I was a dog. Not proud of it, but I was."

"I thought my dad—I mean, Trey—was your friend."

"Porsha, I don't want you to stop calling Trey your dad. He's raised you. It's clear that he loves you, or he never would have contacted me."

"Are you trying to avoid the question?"

"No, I just want it perfectly clear that you calling Trey *Dad* doesn't bother me. I'm hoping one day, you'll bestow the honor on me and call me dad as well."

"A girl can't have two dads."

"Who said they couldn't? Well, you, my dear, do and hopefully, you'll see that."

~ 24 ~

Dion never answered my question about how he could betray his friend, but I didn't press him to do so either. We talked for a few more minutes before my mom made an excuse to come back outside.

"Dear, we need to meet your father at six so, Dion, another time. Maybe."

"Next time, I would like to see Porsha by myself. You don't always have to be present."

"For now, maybe I should be here."

"Mom, it's okay. We've talked. I think it'll be all right."

"Okay. Fine. Whatever. When do you want to see her again?" my mom asked, holding on to her purse tightly.

"Next weekend, if that's okay." Dion looked at me.

My mom responded, "Uh, this can't be an every weekend thing. We do have a family too, you know."

"Not every weekend but at least every other weekend, until we get comfortable with one another."

"Maybe once a month."

"Every other weekend," he insisted.

"People, I'm standing right here. I'm not a six-year-old. I'm about to be sixteen," I yelled.

"What do you want to do?" Dion asked.

"I don't know. Let's play it by ear. I want to go to a basketball game Friday, so can you pick me up Saturday instead?" I asked.

"Saturday morning, it is," he agreed.

"Now that we have that out of the way, let's go, Porsha."

"Yes, ma'am."

"Porsha, you can call me during the week if you like. Anytime."

"Okay, Dion. I'll call you if I feel like talking."

I walked back in the house to go through the front door.

My mom was fast on my heels. "Slow down," she said.

"Well, you were the one who was ready to go," I said.

She turned the alarm on the car off, and we both got in the car.

"We really don't have to meet Trey. I was just rescuing you," my mom said.

"I didn't need rescuing. We were actually having a nice conversation."

"Oh, really?" She sounded disappointed.

I hated it for her, but it wasn't my fault she found herself in this situation. She got on me about being honest, when she had been lying to me all my life.

Once we got back home, I wanted to be by myself, so I went to my room and closed the door. Cole called several times, and so did Danielle and Tara. I avoided all of their calls until later that night. I sent everybody a text saying I wasn't feeling well and that I would see them all at school. Cole didn't sound too pleased with my response, but oh well . . . I wasn't in the mood to explain my situation to him. Maybe tomorrow, but tonight I needed to spend time by myself—me and my thoughts.

My mind tried to figure out the puzzle of my life. Dion seemed okay with me calling Trey *Dad*. Trey seemed okay with me wanting to get to know Dion. My mom didn't seem too happy about it but was only going along with the program because she'd messed up by keeping a huge secret. I could have an attitude with Dion about everything, but he didn't know I existed. He seemed to want a relationship with me.

Brenda, my elder half-sister, seemed cool, although she'd only said a few words to me, but Jasmine had been a jerk ever since I'd known her, so nothing new there.

My life was like a real-life soap opera. Would the drama ever end? Only time would tell, but for now, I needed to get some sleep because no telling what the week ahead would bring.

The next morning, I wanted to be anywhere but school. Cole insisted on walking me to class. I didn't talk much, so he asked me what was bothering me.

"I'll tell you later," I responded. "Some family stuff."

"I'm here if you need to talk," he assured me.

He was so sweet. I just didn't feel like going into it with him right now. It was hard enough concentrating in class. Danielle and Tara each slipped me letters in between classes. Both were inquiring about my meeting with Dion.

Lunch time came quick, especially since I was dreading telling Danielle and Tara what happened.

I was barely seated when Danielle said, "Spill it. We've been waiting on the juice all day."

"I have the new chocolate mousse lip gloss," Tara said, trying to bribe me.

"Although bribes are not necessary, I will take that lip gloss."

Tara handed me the tube.

I recounted the events that took place on Sunday.

"Speaking of drama queen, there she goes there."

Tara looked toward the door.

"And her two friends are with her," Danielle added.

Jasmine walked toward our table with Britney Franklin and Sierra Sanchez in tow. "Can I talk to my sister alone please?" she said, emphasizing the word *sister*.

Danielle and Tara looked at me.

"It's cool," Danielle said. "Let's go outside in the hallway."

I got up from the table, and Jasmine and her friends followed. I turned toward Jasmine. "I thought you said *alone*."

Jasmine whispered something to them, and they both retreated back into the cafeteria. "You'll never be a McNeil," Jasmine said, as she leaned on the wall.

"I don't want to be," I responded. "I'm a Swint, and happy about it."

"Well, regardless of what my dad says, I'll never accept you as my sister."

"You don't have to accept me. I am what I am, so get over it."

"You think you can just come into my life and ruin it, don't you? First you got my boyfriend, and now you're trying to steal my dad away from me. I'm not having it."

Jasmine was really getting on my nerves with her whiny behavior. I walked up a little closer to her because I really didn't want passers-by all up in our business. "Look, I didn't ask for this. It was thrown at me, just like it was thrown at you. We're sisters, and there's nothing you can do about it. Deal with it."

"Cole will never love you like he loved me."

"I suggest you keep Cole's name out of your mouth. What's between us is between us. And this thing about me stealing your dad, I'm the one who should be mad. You've had him all to yourself for fifteen years. Well, move over, *chica*, because I'm here now and I want some of our dad's attention."

"He'll never love you like he loves me," Jasmine shouted before storming away.

Her words vibrated in my head.

~ 25 ~

Later that evening I told my mom about the confrontation with Jasmine.

She said, "I want you to stay clear of that child. She has the same issues as her mama. She's crazy."

"But she's my sister, and you told me I'm to get along with my siblings."

"Well, you might have to make one exception. She has no right stepping to you like that. I'm going to call her mama and set some things straight."

"No, Mom, don't do that. It'll only make things worse."

"Something needs to be done. If she approaches you again, let me know. In fact, call Dion and let him know what his other daughter is doing."

Hmm. That sounded like a good idea. Since Jasmine wanted to step to me the way she did, I'd have to prove to her that Dion could love me just as much as he loved her. While proving it to Jasmine, I would also be proving it to myself, although I wasn't ready to admit that.

I pulled out the card Dion had given me and dialed his number.

"Dion, it's me, Porsha."

"Porsha, I'll have to lock in your number. I have to admit, I'm surprised to hear from you so soon."

"You did say I could call you for anything, right?"

"Why? Of course, dear. What's on your mind?"

I told him about Jasmine's behavior earlier, and he sounded as upset as my mom was.

"Porsha, don't worry about Jasmine. I will deal with her. In fact, she needs to apologize."

"Oh no, she doesn't owe me an apology. I know finding out you have a sister must be real traumatic for her." I was playing the dutiful new daughter role real well. *Little Miss Jasmine better watch out before I have her written out of his will. Okay, that's going a little too far, but she better chill before she alienates the daddy she's loved her whole life.*

Less than thirty minutes later, Dion called me back. "I talked to Jasmine, and you won't be having that problem with her again, she's assured me."

"Thanks, Dion." I made sure I sounded real cheerful. "Well, I got homework. I'll talk to you later."

"Okay, sweetheart. And I'm so glad you called me."

We hung up the phone. Schoolwork was no longer on my mind. Instead, I surfed the Internet and downloaded books on my e-reader.

Jay and Jason were their usual bratty selves over dinner. My mom had us spoiled. The only chores I had were to make sure I kept my room and bathroom clean. I didn't have to wash dishes unless I was in trouble.

For some reason I was in the mood to wash dishes tonight, anything to avoid having to do homework. Ever since finding out about Dion, my grade point average was no longer a top priority for me. All this drama and I was only fifteen. What was the world coming to?

My mom and dad sat at the kitchen table and talked while I washed and put up dishes.

"I'm so proud of how our baby's handling everything," my mom said.

"Yes, she's being very mature about things," my dad added.

"Unlike Jasmine," I chimed in.

"Jasmine will come around. Just wait and see," my dad said.

"I'm not so sure about that. She has a lot of Kim's traits." Mom sipped on her cold drink.

"Give it some time. If she doesn't, that's on her. Just don't be mean to her."

"She better stay out of my way then," I said as I continued to wash dishes.

"We're going to stay out of it. Let the kids handle it themselves," my mom addressed my dad.

They left the kitchen leaving me alone with my thoughts. Justin Bieber's "Baby" ringtone sounded. It alerted me that Cole was on the other end. I wiped my hand on the dishtowel and hit the on button on the touch screen of the phone.

"Are you ready to tell me what's bothering you?" Cole asked.

He had only known me a short time, but he could already pick up on my mood swings. I could tell I was going to like Cole more and more with each new thing he showed me.

My mind flashed back to what Jasmine had said earlier. "Did you ever go out with Jasmine McNeil?" I asked.

"We went out once or twice. Well, maybe three times max, I swear."

"She claims you were her boyfriend."

"I never asked her to be my girl. I found her too much of a drama princess. She's nothing like you," he said.

"Well, we're more alike than you'll ever know," I said.

"What do you mean?" he asked hesitantly.

"She's my sister. My half-sister. We have the same dad."

"Trey Swint is Jasmine's dad. Wow!"

"No, Trey is not her dad."

"Well, I'm confused. You just said you two had the same dad."

"We do. Dion McNeil is my biological father. Trey is my dad."

"Wow! I didn't know that."

"Neither did I until recently."

I told him about our family drama.

"Now, that's reality TV for you," he commented.

"So, are you sure you still want to be my boyfriend?"

"Of course. Who knew you had two great dads?"

"Okay, if I didn't know any better, you're in love with who my dads are."

"Porsha, I'm in love with you, not your dad. Or should I say, dads?"

Did he just say *love*? Oh my goodness. It was love at first sight for him too. *Breathe*, I kept telling myself. *Breathe*. "Cole, it's getting late. I really need to get me some sleep."

"Why you rushing me off the phone?" he asked.

"Because you're delusional. We haven't known each other long enough for you to be 'in love' with me."

"I've loved you from the day I met you. I was just too shy to approach you."

Cole's words left a lasting impression in my mind as I drifted off to sleep.

~ 26 ~

Life seemed better to me in the morning. When I thought about it, my parents were getting along, my new dad was going to pick me up this weekend, and my boyfriend confessed he'd been in love with me for a very long time. After things being mixed up for so long, they suddenly began to look like they were okay. Being at school this morning didn't seem like a chore. I wanted to be there, so I could see Cole.

Cole wasn't standing near the front of the school like he normally was, so I went inside the school and headed toward my homeroom class. I pulled out my cell phone and sent Cole a quick text message alerting him that I was at school.

Stop the presses. I know my eyes didn't see what they were seeing.

I stopped in mid-step as I saw Jasmine kiss Cole or Cole kiss Jasmine. The fact was, their lips were touching. Their lips had no business touching. Cole had just informed me he loved me, and like a fool, I believed him. Not even a good twenty-four hours later, he was locking lips with my sister.

My head started spinning as I felt my breakfast rise up toward my throat. I rushed to the bathroom and released. Afterward I cleaned myself up. I patted myself with a wet paper towel.

When I returned to the hallway, most of the students were already gone to their classes. I slipped in the classroom seconds before my teacher. I barely paid attention to what was being said. All I could think of was the scene that played out earlier. I felt my heart crumbling in two in a matter of seconds.

"Porsha," Cole called out, as I was leaving class.

I ignored him and walked in the opposite direction.

"Wait up. I waited for you this morning, but you never came," he said, once he caught up with me.

"I came and I saw," I responded, not once stopping.

Cole ran and jumped in front of me. "It's not what it seemed like."

I used the palm of my hand and hit my forehead. "Do I have Dumbo the fool plastered on my forehead? I don't think so."

"Jasmine kissed me. I didn't kiss her."

"You could have stopped her," I responded.

"If you were watching, you should have seen me push her off me."

My eyes were glued on the kiss. I didn't see him push her. Did he push her? My memory couldn't compute the information. "Whatever. It shouldn't have happened. It did, and now we're through."

"But, Porsha, I swear I didn't kiss her. I don't want Jasmine, I want you," he yelled.

Other students turned to look in our direction. Embarrassed, I pushed him out of the way and continued to my class.

"Porsha," he yelled out once more.

I could hear my cell phone vibrating in my backpack, so when I got to the classroom, I snuck and checked it. There were several messages from Danielle and Tara asking about the 411 on Cole and Jasmine. It didn't take long for things to get around school. I sent them a quick text saying, Nothing. Before I could turn my phone off, Cole sent me a message saying he was sorry and he wanted to talk. I ignored him.

My stomach was empty, so I couldn't wait for lunch. I almost turned around and left out when I saw my two besties sitting with Cole and Eric.

"What is he doing here?" I asked as I placed my tray on the table.

"Porsha, please talk to me."

"We don't have anything to say to one another," I assured him.

"Give him a chance," Danielle said.

"Dani, I suggest you stay out of our business."

"Excuse me," she responded. She went back to talking to Eric and Tara.

"Jasmine saw you coming. She told me what she was going to do, and I should have walked away then. Before I knew it, she had me in a lip-lock. That's the truth. The God-honest truth," he blurted.

A part of me believed him, but I wasn't going to let him off that easy. "Fine, but you didn't have to kiss her back."

"I didn't kiss her back. I pushed her. Ask Eric. He was right there."

"Eric, did Cole push Jasmine?"

"Well, not really push her, but he did try to make her stop, and she refused," Eric stated.

I was fuming mad inside. Jasmine wanted to play games. I would show her how to play. Don't nobody mess with my emotions and get away with it. Cole should have done more to stop Jasmine. I would forgive him this time, but if I ever caught them in a compromising position again, Cole would have hell to pay.

"So do you forgive me?" he asked.

"I'll think about it." I took a bite out of my sandwich.

"I'll do whatever I can to make it up to you," he said.

"Good. Well, I need a ride to the mall Thursday. Can you take me?"

"I have practice Thursday after school."

"Oh well, I'll find someone else then."

"I can take you around six. Can you stay around until then?"

"Nope. I don't need to go to the mall. I was just testing you."

Cole pled with me the rest of lunch. I gave him a hard time because right then I just wasn't feeling him. He made it his mission to walk me to my next class. Jasmine and her friends were standing near one of the lockers as we walked by.

I said I wasn't going to say anything to her, but as we were passing by, Jasmine said, "Look at her with my leftovers." She laughed loud.

I stopped in mid-step, turned and faced her. "Jealousy is an ugly color on you, sister."

"Sister?" Britney asked.

"Yes, sisters. She didn't tell you? Her and I have the same dad, and I'm the oldest." I smiled, turned around and continued to walk with Cole right on my heels.

Jasmine shouted some obscenities.

"I take it they didn't know," Cole stated.

"Apparently not."

~ 27 ~

Danielle and Tara laughed when I told them about the hallway incident with Jasmine. My mom didn't.

"I hate the day I slept with Dion."

"Well, thanks, Mom."

"No, baby girl, not because of you. I wouldn't trade you for the world. I wish Trey was your biological father. That way you wouldn't have to deal with the likes of Jasmine."

"You and me both," I said. The old feelings of anger were returning. If my mom hadn't slept with Dion, my life wouldn't be spiraling out of control. I frowned.

"What's wrong, dear?" she asked.

"Nothing," I lied. I wanted to get as far away from my mom as possible before I said something that would land me in hot water. "I need to get back to my homework."

Once again, homework was the last thing on my mind. I had a dilemma, and her name was

Jasmine. She would pay for trying to get between me and my man. I needed reinforcements. I got Danielle and Tara on the three-way.

"Jasmine is always in Cole's face, and something needs to be done about it," I said, teeth clenched.

"Forget her," Danielle said. "He's your boyfriend."

"She needs to act like it."

Danielle said, "I can see why she has a crush on him. He's perfect."

"He's great, but he's not perfect. If he was perfect, I wouldn't have caught her kissing him. He would have pushed her away as soon as she even looked like she wanted to kiss him."

Tara stated, "What if Cole secretly does have a crush on Jasmine?"

"Please. Cole is all about our girl. You can tell."

"I hope so. Tara could be right. Maybe he likes the drama," I said, as I scrolled through the Internet.

Danielle said, "No, his friend Eric says Cole is crazy about you. You're all he talks about."

I smiled. That made me feel good that Cole was talking to his friends about me. Maybe I was overreacting to the situation, but then again, what if I wasn't?

"So what's up? How do you plan on making Jasmine pay?" Tara asked.

Tara didn't instigate, but she would follow along with any plans Danielle or I came up with.

"I don't know. That's why I called you two. I need to figure out how to get her to leave my man alone."

My mom walked in on the tail end of our conversation. "Porsha, we need to talk."

"Got to go. My mom just walked in." I disconnected the phone and gave my mom my undivided attention.

"Who are you trying to get to leave your boyfriend alone? Because one thing you should never do is fight another girl over a boy," my mom said, as she took a seat on my bed.

My mom was invading my privacy. I knew she didn't like Jasmine, but I contemplated on whether to give her more details than what she'd overheard. I owed Jasmine no loyalty so I said, "Jasmine is going after my boyfriend, and she knows he's my boyfriend."

"Well, dear, if this Cole guy is entertaining Jasmine and her advances, then he's really not a boy you would want to be with anyway. Sisters should never date the same guy."

I felt myself defending Cole. "It's not like they were ever boyfriend or girlfriend. He said they went out a few times, and that was it. Jasmine has it in her mind that he's hers. Well, he likes me, and he's my boyfriend, so she should be the one to step back."

"You're absolutely right. She needs to. I owe Kim a phone call. She needs to do something about her daughter."

This time I didn't try to talk Mom out of it.

She reached for the cordless phone. "Funny. I remember her number after all these years."

I patted my foot as I watched Mom wait on Jasmine's mom to answer her phone.

"Kim, this is Angie. Give me a call at 972-555-8252 when you get this message. It's about our girls." Mom hung up and then turned and looked at me. "I promise to get to the bottom of this."

If my mom could do that, then maybe I would stop being so angry with her. My emotions were all over the place. One minute things were fine between us, and then the next I wanted to lash out at my mom for lying to me for all these years.

Cole blew my phone up with text messages when I wouldn't answer his numerous phone calls. I wasn't in the mood to talk to him. He would see me at school tomorrow. Until then, sleep was calling my name. I turned my phone on silent and went to bed.

***

I avoided Cole for the remainder of the week. I didn't even go to his game. Later that Friday night, he called me venting. "Porsha, you have to forgive me. I can't sleep. I can't eat. I sucked at tonight's game."

"What does that have to do with me?" I asked, feeling a little smug as I flipped channels on the television while talking to him.

"I'm crazy about you, girl. Can't you see that?" Cole asked.

"Next time keep girls out of our face, and we won't have this problem."

"Can I see you this weekend?" he asked.

"I'll be at Dion's house this weekend, so that would be no."

"Porsha, we can't keep going on like this. Either you're going to forgive me or not."

"Are you giving me an ultimatum because if you are—"

"No. All I'm saying, baby, is, in order for this to work, you have to forgive me. I meant every word I said to you. I love you. You're the first girl I've ever loved."

I threw the remote on the bed and then lay on my stomach. "So, you're telling me you've never felt like this about any other girl?"

"Never. Cross my heart and hope to die."

I responded, "Let's hope it doesn't come to that."

~ 28 ~

"Honey!" Mom yelled from downstairs. "Dion's here!"

I checked my suitcase once more to see if I had everything. I picked up my suitcase and purse with my sweaty palms and headed out of my room.

My dad was in the hallway. "I got it," he said.

Dion and my mom were chatting when we reached the bottom of the stairs. "Are you all ready to go?" he asked.

My dad handed Dion my suitcase. "Someone should be here around six tomorrow."

"I'll have her back by then," Dion assured them.

I hugged them both.

My dad said, "Call me, if you need me."

"She'll be fine," Dion said.

My parents watched us from the doorway as we pulled away. I glanced back at my house as I started a new chapter in my life.

"Are you hungry?" Dion asked.

"Not really," I said, but my stomach was growling, giving me away.

"Seems like your stomach doesn't agree." Dion flashed his beautiful smile, which resembled mine. "How about we stop by and get something real quick, and we can take it back to the house? I have Betty cooking us a nice dinner."

"Sure." What else was I supposed to say? I was just going along with the program.

"Did you have any more problems with Jasmine?" he asked, while we were sharing fries and eating our hamburgers.

This was where I would have to tread carefully. I wanted Dion to like me and I wanted to get back at Jasmine at the same time. But I didn't want Dion to think I was a troublemaker either. "I think your talk may have worked," I lied.

"Good. Because she's coming over later and I want you two to get along."

Say what? Jasmine was the last person I wanted to spend my weekend with.

"I thought it was just going to be you and me. I really don't want to share my time with anyone right now." *Please, please*, I said to myself, *let him agree.*

"Let me call her. I'll get her the next time you're here."

"Thanks, Dion. This is all new to me and I want to get to know you before trying to get to know Jasmine," I said. "And Brenda." I threw her name in there just to take the attention off me not really wanting Jasmine to come.

"Jasmine, there's been a change of plans. You can come over next weekend," I heard him say from his end of the conversation. "I'll call you later."

"So, Dion, now that it's just me and you, what are we going to talk about?" I asked.

"You and Jasmine are more alike than you know. You're both spoiled."

I pouted. "I don't think we're alike."

"There's nothing wrong with being spoiled. Trey and Angie have taken real good care of you. I'm glad of that."

"My parents are great. Well, when they aren't getting on my nerves."

"Spoken like a true teenager." Dion laughed.

I loved his sense of humor. "I still don't think Jasmine and I are alike."

"I know this is difficult for the two of you. My hope is that you two will become close. I'm going to do what I can to make it happen."

I rolled my eyes. "Good luck."

"You just don't know. I'm Dion McNeil. I make it happen."

I laughed.

We spent the rest of the day talking and laughing. I was enjoying my time with Dion. I still didn't feel comfortable enough calling him Dad or anything, but nevertheless, we were getting to know each other. We both hated chocolate. We both loved salty potato chips. We even had similar taste in music. Because of my mom and dad, I loved "old-school" music.

Dion put in the Dance game on Wii, and I couldn't stop laughing as he tried out some of his dance moves. I was surprised he beat me on a few of the routines.

"I can't believe you beat me," I said, as I plopped on the couch.

"Yes, your old man still has a few moves left in him," he said, as he plopped down next to me.

"I think I'm hungry now," I said.

"Betty should be through by now, so go wash up, and I'll meet you back down here in about fifteen minutes," Dion said.

I went to what he said would be my room and washed up. I eyed my reflection in the mirror. I never thought I would be enjoying time with Dion like this. I didn't want to betray my father. It would hurt him too much. I wouldn't let them know how much fun we had. I would keep that to myself. Just something else I could blame my mom for.

Dion was seated at the table when I arrived back downstairs. I took my seat. After he blessed the food, we dived in. Conversation was light between us.

"How about a movie tonight?" he asked.

"There's a movie that I've been wanting to see."

"After dinner, look it up on the Internet and tell me what time, and we'll go."

"Cool."

Less than thirty minutes later, I was in his den surfing for movie times. I went to search for him. I heard him in an intense conversation with someone on the phone. I remained in the hallway.

"Jasmine, I've told you, your attitude is going to stop you from getting a lot of things."

I wondered what she wanted.

He added, "She's your sister, and she will be a part of my life, whether you like it or not, so you might as well get used to it."

It felt good hearing Dion take up for me. Jasmine didn't seem to be taking our relationship well. Her problem, not mine.

I opted for me and Dion to stay in and watch some of his movies he had on DVD. We watched several comedies and laughed until we both got sleepy. Hanging out with my new dad was fun.

~ 29 ~

"Did you have fun this weekend?" my mom asked me as I was unpacking my clothes.

"It was okay."

"He didn't make you feel uncomfortable or anything?"

"No, of course not. We talked. Watched movies. Ordered pizza."

"Well, that's good. I wanted to talk to him about your party."

My hand flew up to my mouth. "I can't believe I forgot about my party. The invites."

"I saw your list on your desk and took care of it. There's a stack over there you will need to hand-deliver because I don't have their addresses."

"Mom, you're the greatest." I stopped what I was doing and hugged her. Tonight I wasn't mad at her. I slipped the invitations in my backpack.

"Hate to spoil our love fest, but I have one more question I want to ask you."

I dropped my arms to my side. "I'm listening."

"Did you see Jasmine this weekend?"

"No, thank God. She's such a drama queen."

"I know you didn't, Ms. Always-got-drama-going-on."

"But, Mom, seriously, I am not a drama queen."

"Drama princess then."

I rolled my eyes.

My mom laughed. "Dear, although her mom is not one of my favorite people, you should try to get along with her."

I returned to unpacking my suitcase. I mumbled, "I'll try."

"Kim's supposed to stop by tomorrow evening. I've already asked Danielle's mom if she could drop you off."

My mom had my full attention again, but she finished her conversation and left me in my room by myself. Once I had unpacked, I called Cole. I had made him suffer enough.

"I was wondering if you ever were going to call me," he said.

"Told you I was spending time with my new dad this weekend."

"That's still surreal. Finding out the dad you thought was your father really isn't."

"It is what it is," I responded. By then I was sitting on my bed with my legs crossed, filing my fingernails.

"We have another home game this week. Would love it if you would be there," he said.

"Depends on you. If you act right, I'll be there."

"I'll behave. Promise."

I could imagine him smiling. I found myself melting and falling for his boyish charms all over again. "Cole, I'll see you tomorrow. I'm tired. I need to get me some sleep."

"Okay," he said. He sounded disappointed, I was sure he would get over it.

Even with me getting eight hours of sleep, I still overslept. I rushed and got dressed while my mom made sure my brothers were dressed. My dad dropped the boys off, and I rode with my mom. She was quiet, except for the occasional laugh she would get from listening to the *Tom Joyner Morning Show*. I liked listening to Rickey Smiley, but since I wasn't in my own car yet, I enjoyed the old-school music my mom listened to every morning.

"Looks like you have an admirer," my mom said, as I retrieved my backpack from the backseat of the car.

I turned around to look. It was Cole. He waved. "That's just Cole," I responded.

"Ask him to come here. I would love to meet him."

"Mom, not now. Maybe later."

"Now!"

"Ugh! Okay." I walked up to where Cole stood. "My mom wants to meet you."

"Cool." He almost bumped me out of the way to get to the car. "Hi, Mrs. Swint. It's a pleasure to meet you."

My mom stuck her hand out the window and shook his. "Nice to meet you too, Cole. Cole, what's your parents, name?"

"Mom," I said from behind.

Cole said, "I don't mind. My mom's name is Freda Baylor. She's a nurse. My dad's dead. He died when I was young."

"Sorry to hear that. Well, we'll have to have you and your mom over for dinner one night."

"I'm sure she'll like that."

The first bell was ringing in the distance. "Mom, that's the bell. We should get going."

"Don't forget you're riding with Danielle this evening," she reminded me.

"Your mom seems cool," Cole said, as we walked toward the school.

"She's all right when she's not getting on my nerves," I said.

"She seems down-to-earth."

"She is. You don't have to lay the compliments on thick. We're cool, all right."

"Oh, I wasn't trying to suck up to you." He flashed his Colgate smile. "Then again, I can stand to get all the brownie points I can get." He pulled a box out of his pocket.

"What's this?" I asked, as he opened it.

"I want you to wear my ring. You're my girl, and I want the whole world to know it." He retrieved a gold necklace with his class ring attached to it from the box.

"Cole, this is serious. Are you sure?" I asked. We were now standing near my homeroom.

"I'm positive. Turn around."

I did as I was told. I moved my hair out of the way as he placed the necklace around my neck. Several people walking by noticed the exchange. It was official. Everyone would know by the end of the day that Cole and I were an item.

Jasmine, eat your heart out.

~ 30 ~

At lunch, I handed Danielle and Tara their invitations.

Danielle opened up hers. "Girl, you're having your party at Southfork Ranch."

"Hee haw!" Tara shouted out. "I love horses."

Say what? I hadn't even looked at the invitations. I just assumed the party was going to be at our house. I had no idea my party was at Southfork. I took the cowboy-shaped paper from Danielle's hand and read it out loud:

"The pre-party starts at four. Be prepared to ride horses and participate in some fun games. The after-party starts at promptly seven o'clock. Bring a change of clothes—dress to impress— formal wear only. Since this is a masquerade ball, masks will be provided. R.S.V.P. Envelope enclosed."

"This is going to be so cool. I haven't rode horses since I was a little girl," Tara said.

Danielle and I looked at her. I was the first to speak. "You were a little girl like yesterday, duh."

"You know what I meant." She looked a little teary-eyed.

"Your party is going to be different. I love it." Danielle commented.

My party was going to be a cross between a picnic and a masquerade ball, a whole day and night of fun. The countdown was on.

I gave Danielle and Tara each some invitations to pass out for me. I glanced at one of the envelopes and started to trash it, but I knew my mom would've asked me if I gave it to her, so I set out on a mission to locate my crazy half-sister.

She was looking sad. I almost felt sorry for her, well, that is until she looked up and opened her mouth.

"What do you want?" she asked.

I reached in my bag and pulled out the envelope. "I wanted to give you this."

She snatched it from my hand. I was inches away from snatching her hair.

"If it's about your stupid party, I doubt if I'll be able to come. I have something to do that weekend."

***

I shrugged my shoulders. "Fine with me. I didn't want you there anyway."

"In that case, I'll make sure I'm there." She threw the invitation in her purse.

"You're pathetic."

"No, you're the pathetic one, trying to be all up in my dad's face. If he only knew how evil you really were," Jasmine said.

I laughed. Jasmine was a joke. I was not going there with her. I walked away.

"Don't walk away from me," she yelled.

Britney called out to her. "Jas, you need to get a grip."

"She's ruining my life," I heard Jasmine said.

A smile filled my face. "Like you tried to ruin mine," I responded out loud as I continued to my class.

Between my two best friends and me, we handed out all of the invitations to my sweet sixteen party. Everybody who got one seemed to be as excited as I was about it. The only damper would be seeing Jasmine. I was hoping she'd change her mind, but my gut feeling told me she would be there, if only to make my life miserable.

My hand kept fidgeting with the necklace round my neck. Being Cole's girl made me feel special. I had never been in love before, so whatever I was feeling was foreign to me.

Cole stood at the water fountain after school waiting for me. "I know you're supposed to be riding with Danielle, but I don't have practice today. Coach cancelled. I can drive you home."

"I'm not so sure about that. My mom's real strict about stuff."

"Come on. We'll go straight to your house. Scout's honor." He crossed his chest and held up two fingers.

"I didn't know you were a Boy Scout."

"I'm not."

I playfully hit him.

He laughed. "So, please?" He batted his eyelashes.

"I'll tell Danielle I got another ride home."

Danielle walked up to us. "You ready?"

"Cole's going to drop me off."

"You sure? You don't want your mama tripping this close to your party."

"What party?" Cole asked.

"We'll talk about it in the car," I said. "Tell your mama whatever. I'm riding with Cole." I turned back to face Cole. "Come on. Where are you parked?"

"On the east side," he said, as we walked away from Danielle.

I trusted Danielle not to reveal that Cole was taking me home, because her mom would surely call my mom if she did. Once in Cole's car, I sent Danielle a text message just to make sure.

"Cole, back to the party. You automatically get an invite because you're my boyfriend. Things have been so hectic, I just hadn't had time to talk to you about it."

"Of course, I'm your date."

We rapped along with Lil Wayne's latest CD. By the time we got to my favorite song, Cole was pulling up in front of my house. I noticed a strange car and remembered Jasmine's mom was supposed to meet up with my mom. I was in no rush to go inside.

"Cole, why didn't you tell me your dad was dead?" I asked.

"My stepdad is like my dad, so it wasn't like I was trying to keep secrets from you."

"Well, please don't. I've had enough people doing that." I was thinking about my mom.

"Everybody at school has been talking about us, you know." He reached over and grabbed my hand, and our fingers interlocked.

"Really? What are they saying?"

"That we make a cute couple. How they are surprised I finally have a girlfriend."

"You're not one of them *D-L* brothers, are you?" I'd heard my mom and friends talk about men who were on the down low and didn't tell their spouses. I wanted to know if Cole was secretly gay and was just using me as a smoke screen.

"No. I'm one hundred percent heterosexual male."

Whew! "Glad to know. Otherwise, we were going to have a serious problem."

After Cole and I had been sitting in the car for ten minutes, I told him, "Cole, I better go before my mom starts calling around looking for me. Thanks for the ride home."

"Anytime I don't have practice, I can drop you off," he said.

"I'll have to remember that. Later, 'gator."

I used my key to enter the house. I heard my mom and somebody talking. My guess was, it was Jasmine's mom. The voices were coming from the living room. Apparently, they were unaware that I was at home because their conversation didn't cease. In fact, their voices got a little louder. Once again, I found myself eavesdropping.

"I never meant to hurt you. I really didn't, Kim," my mom said.

"Angie, I forgave you a long time ago, but seeing you and your daughter the other week just drug up old memories. Memories that I thought

I had suppressed." She paused before adding, "I'm not putting all the blame on you. I know Dion was the one I was married to."

"Dion was manipulative," my mom said. "He took advantage of me. He knew how much I was hurting over Trey."

"Dion was fine back in the day. I don't know one woman who didn't want him."

"Believe it or not, I was one of those women. He just caught me at a weak moment. He said the right words. I needed to feel loved. If it hadn't been Dion, it would have been any other guy at that point in my life."

Wow! I couldn't believe my mom admitted that.

Kim went on to say, "I will try to talk to Jasmine, but Dion hurt her with this new revelation. She took our divorce pretty hard, you know."

"I admit, I did watch your show. Just to be nosy."

Sounded like our mothers were making amends. I wondered if Jasmine and I could ever reach that point. Only time would tell. For now, I had to use the bathroom, so I cleared my throat and entered the living room.

"Hi, Mom," I said, as I went and hugged her. I turned and looked at Jasmine's mom. "Hi, Ms. Kim."

"Porsha, good to see you." She stood up. "Well, Angie, I better get going. We'll be in touch."

"Let me walk you out." My mom stood up and followed Jasmine's mom to the front door.

My bladder refused to wait for me to go upstairs, so while my mom was walking Kimberly out, I hightailed it to the downstairs bathroom.

My mom was seated in the living room when I made it out. "So how much did you overhear?" she asked.

I opened up my mouth to lie but hesitated. "Not much."

"She's promised to talk to Jasmine, and I agreed to do the same with you." She patted the sofa near her. "Come sit."

"Mom, I have a lot of homework to do." I wasn't concerned with homework. I was only concerned with avoiding wherever this conversation was headed.

"It can wait."

I reluctantly sat next to her.

She looked at me. "Dear, although Kim and I are having our issues, we both agreed that you and Jasmine are sisters and should try to work on your relationship."

"We've already discussed this," I said.

"Well, we've thought about doing a spa day this Saturday. Just the five of us."

"Five?"

"Yes, your sister Brenda is eager to learn more about you."

"Really?" That was good to hear. I would call Dion and get Brenda's phone number. Having an older sister would be cool.

"So you and Kim McNeil are willing to put your problems aside so that we can get along. Is that what you're saying?" I asked.

"Sort of. We still have a long ways to go, but at least we're not threatening to hurt one another, like in the past."

"Mom, can we put off the spa day until after my party. My party is two weeks away."

"No, because I want you two at least on speaking terms by your party."

When my mom was in this mode, there was no talking her out of it. She went on and on about the importance of family. Dare I remind her, my family wouldn't be so messed up if she hadn't lied. I was beginning to sound like a broken record here, and so was she. "All I can promise you is that I will try. Now, can I be excused?"

"Go ahead. You're just as stubborn as your father," she said.

"Which one?"

"Both of them."

"Whatever," I said under my breath, grabbing my backpack and heading upstairs.

I logged on to the computer and entered Danielle, Tara, and my private chat area. Both were sitting idle until I sent a message. "We're having a spa day. I don't want to go."

"Then I'll go in your place," Tara typed. "My little brother and sister are getting on my nerves. My mom's going out of town again this weekend, and of course, I got babysitting duty."

The next five minutes we chatted about Tara's problem. Momentarily, I forgot about mine. Danielle sent a link for me to click on and marked it "urgent."

"What is it?" I asked before clicking.

"I'll call you," she typed as her response.

While waiting for her to call, I clicked on the link. A picture of Dion, Kim, Jasmine and Brenda stared back at me. But what really got my attention was the caption. "DID DION HAVE AN OUTSIDE LOVE CHILD?"

Danielle was on the phone before I could read any more. "Did you click on it?"

"Yes. Wait. I'm reading it."

The article read: *Sources revealed National Sports Caster and former NFL Star Dion McNeil has a secret child. The child is said to be another daughter around the same age as his youngest. Since Dion was still married at that time, it means that he was double-dipping. Details to follow. As soon as we know, you'll know.*

"Before you even think it, I did not tell anyone about this," Danielle said.

"Did you tell your mama?" I asked.

"She doesn't count," she responded.

I typed a quick message to Tara. Tara responded that she hadn't told anyone either.

"Maybe it was someone at the doctor's office you went to," Danielle suggested.

Tara sent me another link while I was talking to Danielle. I clicked on it, and there was my mom's face for the whole world to see.

Just when I thought things couldn't get any worse, they did.

"Jasmine has probably been running her mouth," I said out loud.

~ 32 ~

I hung up with Danielle and ran to locate my mom. "Mama, Mama," I yelled out.

"Girl, I'm in the kitchen. Stop all that yelling."

"Look at this." I pulled up the link on my iPhone and handed it to her.

"I bet you that skank did this to try to embarrass me. Here I thought we were making amends," my mom said, as she handed me back the phone.

"How am I supposed to go to school tomorrow? Everybody will be talking about it. I can't show my face there ever again." The blood vessels in my head pounded like a sledge hammer.

"Calm down, dear. It's not that serious. I'll get a PR person on this right away."

My mom left the kitchen to make some phone calls while I was left trying to figure out how I was going to deal with my business all out in the streets for everyone to see. I had planned on introducing Dion as my dad at my sweet sixteen

party. Not like this. Now people would be looking at me strange. The article made my mom
sound like a home-wrecker.

*Oh, my. What would my dad think when he
finds out?* I got all of this drama going on, and I
hadn't even made sixteen yet.

"Kim said she didn't know anything about it."
My mom had re-entered the kitchen with her
phone glued to her ear. "Leslie, I need for you to
come over here as soon as you can."

I couldn't hear what Leslie was saying, but apparently she agreed.

"I got to call Trey. Man, this is getting out of
control," she said.

The door opened, and Jay and Jason ran in,
making a lot of noise. My dad was behind them.
"What's wrong with my girls?" he said. "You two
look like death on a stick."

I looked at my mom, and she looked at me.

"Jay and Jason, come on, let's go upstairs for
a minute," I said.

"For what?" Jay asked.

"Come on. Can't you see they want some privacy?" Jason pointed at Mom and Dad.

Once I made sure they were upstairs in their
room playing a video game, I eased back down
the stairway and stood outside of the kitchen
door.

"Leslie's on her way over here. You can stop yelling," Mom said.

"This is what I wanted to avoid. I don't want our baby's name in the news."

"Baby, it's been leaked. I need to make a statement. Take the gossip out of it and just address it and not avoid it."

"No wonder my phone's been ringing off the hook. I've just been too busy today to talk to anyone if it wasn't you or the kids. Have you talked to Dion?" he asked.

"You know what. It probably was him. He's probably trying to garner up ratings for his show."

"Don't bother. I'm calling him now."

I tiptoed back upstairs. I did a quick search and clicked on the different links talking about Dion McNeil. One website swore it was a love triangle between Dion, Mom, and Dad. My cell phone beeped to indicate I had missed calls and messages. Several people from school were calling me, including Cole. I deleted the messages and dialed Cole's number. When his phone went to voice mail, I hung up without leaving a message.

Dion's number popped up on my cell phone. I answered.

"Are you all right?" he asked.

"Yes, sir," I responded.

"We're going to get to the bottom of this. Talking about me is one thing, but bringing my kids into it is something else. Don't you worry about it. And hold your head up high. You have nothing to be ashamed about."

His phone beeped. "That's Jasmine on the other end. Call me if you need me, okay."

"I'm fine," I said.

My mom entered my room without knocking like she normally did. "Did Dion call you like he said he would?"

"I just hung up with him."

"Nobody seems to know how all of this was leaked. He's going to contact the doctor's office tomorrow. If we find out they leaked it, they will be sued." She walked near me and wrapped her arms around me. "It's going to be okay, baby," she said.

"I'm still not going to school tomorrow."

"Things will look brighter in the morning."

The doorbell rang.

"That's probably Leslie. Get you some rest. I'll be dropping you off at school tomorrow."

I waited upstairs as long as I could. I had to know what was going on and being said, so I headed downstairs.

Jay said from behind me. "Mama told us to stay up here."

"She said *y'all* stay up here. She didn't give me the same orders," I responded.

"I'm telling Mama," Jay yelled.

"You better not open your mouth." I gave him the evil eye, and he retreated back to his room.

Fooling with Jay made me miss the first part of their conversation. By the time I entered the hallway near the living room, they were talking about what my mom would say to the media if anyone contacted her.

Leslie said, "You can direct all media questions to me. This is not a bad thing at all. You've been thinking about launching your new jewelry, so now is the time to capitalize on the attention and bring the conversation back to it."

"But isn't that tacky?" Mom asked.

"It's called turning negative press into positive press, and any time it can put money in your pocket, it's positive, right?"

"Right about that."

"Young lady," my dad said from behind me, causing me to jump, "you're going to get tired of eavesdropping."

"I—I didn't want to interrupt," I stuttered.

He laughed. "Just like your mama."

"She said I'm just like you."

"Well, then you're all right, kid." He smiled.

I smiled back and headed back toward the stairs.

~ 33 ~

Who would have thought news of me being Dion McNeil's daughter could cause this much of a commotion? We arrived at school and saw news crews from local and national stations camped outside.

"See? Told you I should have stayed at home," I said.

Mom said, "Oh, you're going to school. I'm going to drive around back, and you can go through the cafeteria."

After my cloak-and-dagger move, I entered the school through the back door. People who knew who I was stared at me as I walked down the hallway. I saw several people stop and stare and heard them whisper. I attempted to hold my head up high. I would have been satisfied going back home, but no, my mom insisted that I go to school. I bumped into Cole in the hallway.

"I tried to call you last night," he said.

"I called you back too but got your voice mail," I said.

"I heard about what happened. You all right?"

"Cole, I'm fine. I'd be even better if people would stop asking me that question."

"*Woo!* I'm on your side, remember?"

"Sorry, Cole. I'm under a lot of pressure right now."

Danielle and Tara ran up to us. "Girl, did you see all those news trucks? You're hot news," Tara said.

"I wish folks would just stay out of my business and mind their own," I snapped.

I left Cole and my two BFFs staring at my backside as I headed to my homeroom. There was more whispering and murmurs during class. I did my best to ignore them, but it was really grating on my nerves.

"We need to talk," were the words Jasmine blurted out to me when we ran into each other in the hallway.

"I don't know if that's a good idea," I responded.

"I'm used to dealing with the media, and I'm telling you, I think we should."

I thought about it. Jasmine did have her own reality show. I also recalled when her parents were divorcing how the media blew that out of proportion too. It wouldn't hurt to listen to her.

"What do you have to say?"

"All eyes are going to be on us, so I think we should try to have a united front."

"You mean lie," I said, tilting my head.

"We don't have to act like we're best buddies or anything, but at least look like we're happy that we now have each other as sisters."

"You're the actress, not me," I said.

"You're not making this easy for me, are you?" she snapped.

"And you thought I would, after you tried to push up on my boyfriend like you did?" I snapped back.

"I can't help it that your boyfriend wanted some of this." Jasmine ran her hand up and down in front of her body.

I put my hand on my hip. "He couldn't want that, when he has all of this."

"I should have known you wouldn't cooperate. That's okay. I'll get my own reality show another way."

"Snap. You leaked it, didn't you? You're the one who leaked it about me being Dion's daughter. How could you?"

Jasmine walked up near me and grabbed my arm, but I snatched it away from her.

"Please. Let's go in here and talk," she said.

I looked around as some other students gathered around us. They were already in my business too much, so I followed Jasmine into the vacant classroom.

"I had to do something. The producer said my life was a little too boring for its own show. I didn't think it would get out of hand like it did. I pitched an idea about two long-lost sisters."

"Jasmine, what were you thinking? You of all people should know how the media can be, but no, you wanted a reality show. You didn't think about nobody but yourself. Wait until Dion finds out you're the one who leaked this." I rambled through my backpack in search of my phone.

"No, you can't tell Daddy. He'll kill me. This wasn't supposed to be negative publicity, just a way to secure me a reality show."

I laughed. "You're pathetic. You want to be a star that much?"

"I was going to bring you in on the show too. Did you listen to anything I said? A show about two sisters finding their way to each other."

"You're a joke. We don't even like each other, so what makes you think I would do a show with you?"

"One point five million dollars," she blurted.

I stopped looking for my phone. "You got to be kidding me."

"I'm serious. We would get one point five million dollars apiece," she said.

"So when were you going to let me in on this?"

"Well, I really wasn't. I was going to be the star of the show, and you were just going to be a by-product."

I laughed. "You're a piece of work. There's no way in the world I will go along with your madness. As soon as I find my phone, I'm letting Dion know how the media knew about me."

"Please don't tell Dad. I'll do anything. Anything you want," Jasmine pled.

I tilted my head to the side. "Anything?"

"Yes, anything."

"First, you need to back up off Cole, and I mean back, way back."

"But—"

"No, buts."

"Okay. Fine. You can have Cole."

Before I could finish, the principal stuck his head in the room. "Ladies, come with me."

~ 34 ~

This was my first time being summoned to the principal's office. I walked behind him, while Jasmine mumbled something. I ignored her.

Once behind closed doors, the principal sat down behind his desk. "I've called your parents to come get you because the media outlets are disrupting school. Until the media frenzy has died down, I've asked your teachers to e-mail you your assignments."

Jasmine smiled.

I didn't. "Can I come to the game on Friday, or am I suspended from that as well?" I asked.

"For now it's best that you and Jasmine stay clear of school and any of its activities."

I dropped my head down. "This is messed up."

"I'm just trying to do what's best for the majority of the student body. Your parents understand," the principal stated.

"I sure don't," I responded.

Jasmine whispered, "This could be a good thing."

"For you, maybe, but not me. I was scheduled to get my senior ring this Friday. Now I'm going to miss the ceremony."

"We'll have your ring delivered to your house," the principal assured me.

I rolled my eyes. I looked at Jasmine. "Thanks to you, my life is screwed up."

One of the school secretaries knocked on the door.

"Come in," the principal responded.

"Mrs. McNeil is here to pick up the girls."

"Where's my mom?" I asked out loud.

Kim walked from behind the secretary. "Porsha, I talked to your mom. I'm to drop you off at home."

"Thanks . . . I guess," I mumbled.

"We'll see you on Monday," the principal stood up to say.

Jasmine followed Kim out the door. I lagged behind. I could feel my cell phone vibrating in my backpack. While walking, I retrieved it. It was a text from my mom. I didn't respond to it until we were pulling away from the school's campus.

"Porsha, the best advice I can give you about dealing with reporters is to ignore them. Eventually, they will go away," Kim said, as she drove me home. Kim went on and on about how to deal with the media. She was a drama queen.

Now I could see where Jasmine got her actions from. If Jasmine hadn't confessed to leaking the information, I would have thought Kim was behind it. I came very close to asking her if she knew about Jasmine's role in it all.

Jasmine remained quiet for most of the ride to my house. She turned around and handed me a piece of paper. "This is my number. Call me later."

It took me a few seconds to take it from her. Once I did, I placed the paper in my backpack. I leaned back in my seat and looked out of the window the remainder of the trip home.

Of course, when we arrived home, several news media trucks were camped on the street in front of my house. Kim ignored them and drove up the driveway.

"Tell your mom I will call her later," Kim stated, as she parked the car.

"Thanks, Mrs. McNeil," I said, as I released my seatbelt.

"Call me Ms. Kim," she said.

Jasmine said, "Don't forget to call me."

I didn't say a word. I saw cameras flashing as I walked up to the front door. My mom jerked the door open and pulled me inside. She slammed the door. "I should have listened to you. Let you stay at home today."

I dropped the backpack off my shoulder and grabbed the handle of it with my hand. I could have said I told you so, but refrained from doing so. "Why didn't you come get me?" I asked, as we walked to the living room.

"Dion and I talked. Kim happened to be there when the school called. Besides, I had to finalize my press statement with Leslie. She's releasing my statement to the press as we speak."

"What's it going to say?" I asked.

"No need for you to worry. Just know your mama's taken care of everything."

"You might as well tell me. It'll be on one of the gossip sites later, and I'm only going to read it there," I said.

"Look, I don't have time for this," my mom snapped.

"You're the reason why this is going on."

"How long are you going to blame me?" she yelled.

"Until I feel like stopping," I yelled back.

"What's going on here? I can hear you two outside," Dad said, catching us both off guard.

"Daddy." I ran up to him and hugged him.

"Baby girl, it's going to be all right." He held me in his arms.

I played the damsel-in-distress role to the hilt. "I hate I got pulled out of school for this."

"Me too. I will be talking to that principal later on about this. He should have better control over who he lets on campus?

My mom said, "He can't stop them from being on the streets."

"Well, I pay my taxes like everybody else, and my daughter shouldn't have to stay at home because of some nosy reporters. Principal Jackson needs to realize that. You'll be back in school on Monday. Believe that."

"It's best that she stays here. I don't like all of this attention."

"You should have thought of that before." Dad looked at me. "Why don't you go upstairs? I need to talk to your mom."

I grabbed my backpack and looked back at my mom, who looked upset. I didn't care. She brought the drama on herself.

~ 35 ~

"I hope you don't mind, but I got your number from our dad," Jasmine said from the other end of the phone over an hour later.

"I really do mind. I don't feel like talking to you or anyone else," I said.

"Have you decided what you're going to do?"

"No, I haven't." I got out of bed and turned on my computer.

"Whatever you want me to do, I will do it, as long as you don't tell my dad what I did."

"You mean OUR dad, don't you?"

"Yes," Jasmine said barely above a whisper.

"I didn't hear you."

"Yes." This time she said it louder.

"Okay, we've already established that you will stop jumping up in Cole's face. The other thing I want from you is to stop bad-mouthing me to our dad."

"I don't."

"Don't even say it. I know you do."

I put my mom's name in one of the search engines and got a lot of hits.

"Whatever. Either you're going to tell or not. I'm not going to keep going back and forth with you on this."

"I'm telling." I hung the phone up.

Seconds later, Jasmine called me back.

I answered, "What?!"

"I'm sorry, okay. All of this stress is getting to me."

"Me telling Dion what you did won't hurt me. It'll hurt you."

"Please do this for me. We're sisters, remember?"

I could tell she was pouting. "Sisters in name only," I reminded her.

"I'll treat you better," she said.

I laughed. "So if I don't tell our dad about what you did, you promise to treat me better. Wow! You really don't want me to tell now, do you?"

"Promise you won't tell," she begged.

"I'll think about it." Without saying another word, I hung up the phone.

Jasmine called back, and I hit the ignore button. The articles coming up on the computer screen held my attention.

I scrolled through the press release sent out by Leslie on behalf of my mom. My mom admitted that Dion and she shared a child, and asked that their privacy be respected. The comments on the blog pages however were nasty and mean, and some accused my mom of being a home-wrecker. I couldn't understand why, because Dion and Kim had only recently divorced.

It was okay for me to be mad at my mom, but I really didn't like some of the comments I was reading about her. I created a log-in name and responded to some of the comments. I'm sure it didn't make it any better, but at least they would know how I felt. I logged off and lay across my bed.

The knock on the door brought me out of a soft nap.

"Porsha, can we come in?" my dad asked from the other side of the door.

"It's unlocked," I yelled.

Mom and Dad entered, and stood on opposite sides of my bed.

My dad said, "We just read the comment you left on one of the blog sites. Although we appreciate you taking up for Angie, we think it's best that you keep quiet."

I didn't say anything until I noticed my dad unplugging my laptop. "What are you doing?" I asked.

"We're taking your laptop until all of this calms down," my mom said.

"But you can't. That's all I have right now. How am I supposed to get and do my schoolwork?"

"I didn't think about that, dear," Mom said, addressing my dad.

"You can use the laptop in our room when we're there."

I pouted. "Whatever. I was just trying to help."

Mom sat on the edge of my bed. "We know, dear, but we got this. You just worry about school."

I remained silent but was fuming inside. I wasn't a little child, and they needed to stop treating me as such.

Jasmine called me again, and this time I answered.

"'Bout time you answered," she said.

"Look, you need to chill with the attitude."

"So, what do you say? Would you do the reality show with me? It'll help squash all the rumors."

"E-mail me the information." I forgot I didn't have my computer. But, wait a minute, my phone had Internet access.

"Give me a few minutes. Read over it and then call me back and let me know."

I hung up with her. I never thought I would be making a deal with my enemy. My folks had upset me. I had to show them I could make my own decisions. I clicked on the icon sent to me by Jasmine and opened the document. The money and the show became more interesting, the more I read.

I called Jasmine back. "I'll do it. First, I have to convince my mom to let me."

"I'm working on my mom too," she confessed.

I went directly to my parents' room when I hung up with Jasmine.

"Come in," my dad yelled.

"Can I talk to Mom by herself?" I asked.

"I need to go pick up the boys anyway," my dad said. He kissed my mom and hugged me before leaving.

My mom patted for me to sit next to her on the bed. "So, what do you want to talk to me about?" she asked.

"I'm sorry about making things worse by leaving comments." I thought starting with an apology would soften what I was about to say.

"It didn't hurt. It's just I don't want you open for ridicule. It might make me go ghetto on some folks, you know." She laughed.

"Jasmine and I have been talking, and we think we have a solution."

"Say what? I thought you two couldn't stand each other." Mom leaned back to look at me.

"We can't, but we have a workable solution. We want to do a reality show together."

"Have you lost your mind?"

My mother's words rang in my ear as she ranted.

~ 36 ~

It took my mom a few minutes to calm down. "I bet you it was that drama princess idea to do this, wasn't it?"

"Yes, ma'am. But I thought about it. It's a good idea."

"We've been able to keep you sheltered from the media up until this point. I don't think it's a good idea."

"Well, I'll be sixteen next month, and I think I'm old enough to make my own decisions."

"As long as you stay in my house, you will do as I say."

"Maybe I should call Dion and see about moving in with him." I knew I shouldn't have said those words, but she'd made me mad.

The anger on her face was gone. It was replaced with sadness. Tears streamed down my mom's face.

"All we've done for you is love you and gave you the best life we knew possible. Now you want to go live with a man you barely know. I can't stand to look at you right now." She stormed out of the room and headed directly to their master bathroom, slamming the door behind her.

Her words cut me to the core. I sat on her bed waiting and waiting for her to return. Maybe I had gone too far. But I was tired of everyone else around me dictating my life. I eased off the bed, head bowed down, and went back to my room. I wanted to scream, but instead I lay my head on my pillow and cried.

My mom entered the room and sat next to me. She rubbed the back of my head. "This is all my fault. I'm sorry, baby."

I remained quiet.

She continued. "I'll talk to Trey when he gets back, and we'll decide what to do. I don't think allowing you to do a reality show will fly well with him."

I turned over. "Thanks, Mom."

"If it'll bring you and your sister closer, then maybe it is the right thing to do."

I wasn't so sure about the closeness, but it could be interesting. Maybe Jasmine would stop acting so much like a jerk. Maybe we could get past our differences and become more like sisters than enemies.

Once my mom left, I called Jasmine back. I told her, "If my dad approves, I will be able to do it."

"Which dad?" she asked.

"My dad-dad."

"Oh, you mean Trey?"

"Yes, of course."

"Well, I can tell you *our* dad is not going to like it, but since my mom has full-time custody, as long as I can get her to go for it, then he has nothing to say about it."

"So you would do it without his permission?" I asked.

"Sure. I like being in the spotlight. I want to be an actress one day, you know, the next Halle Berry." She went on to say. "He can be cool when he wants to be. One year, he got Trey Songz to sing at my birthday party."

"Really?" My ears perked up because I had a serious crush on Trey Songz.

"I'm going to see him later on today and ask him about it," Jasmine said.

"Maybe you should wait until this mess calms down before approaching him."

"No. Got to do it now because those producers want an answer as soon as possible."

It seemed like Jasmine had all the answers. I had no aspirations of being in entertainment until now. The allure of fame was begging me to enter those doors. *If only my dad would agree and be willing to sign on the dotted line so I could get my own slice of the reality pie.*

I sat in limbo for the rest of the day waiting for my dad's answer to the reality TV offer. He didn't respond during dinner, nor did he say anything to me later on that night. I was beginning to think that Mom hadn't approached him with it. I flipped my light off and surfed the net on my iPhone. I got angrier and angrier as I read some of the message boards about Mom and Dion.

I heard a light knock on my door. "Baby girl, you still up?" Dad opened the door and peeped in.

I flipped my phone over real quick. "I'm up. Just listening to music."

He turned the lamp on near my bed and took a seat in the chair by my desk. "I understand you and your sister want to do a reality show."

"Yes, sir."

"Why do you think I should say yes?" he asked.

"Because it'll give me a chance to tell my side of the story. It'll bring me and my sister closer, and I can make my own money to go toward my college fund," I said with confidence.

"People will think what they want to think regardless of what you say. Being on a reality show isn't the answer to you and Jasmine's problem. Y'all need one-on-one time together. As far as your college fund, I've already taken care of that. I've made sure to put money aside for you to attend any college your heart desires."

"What if I told you I've secretly wanted to be a star, like the Montanas and the Biebers?" I was sitting up now.

"Then if that's what you want, I'll make it happen."

"You've always said I could sing, so yes, I want to do this. I want to use the show to jumpstart me a music career."

"I need the show's information, and I will get my lawyer to handle the details. If everything pans out, then yes, I'll give you my permission to do the show."

I jumped off the bed and hugged him. "Thank you, Daddy."

"Calm down. Your mom has to come on board too. That's the other condition."

I pouted. "Please make her see my side of it."

"For you, I'll do anything."

Once he left, I retrieved my iPhone and looked up Jasmine's number. I sent her a text message.

I'm in. Send me the producers contact info.

Seconds later, I had all the information I needed to give my dad. I sighed. This could be the beginning of an exciting new life for me. I daydreamed about superstardom.

Leslie and my mom did their best to keep the media at bay, but I ended up staying in the house the entire weekend. I was now having second thoughts about the reality show, but Danielle and Tara were excited about it.

"I know you're going to allow me to make a few cameos," Danielle said.

"Of course, she is. We need to be practicing our routines so when they are filming us singing, we will sound all right," Tara stated.

"It's not a done deal yet. I won't know until next week."

"Your birthday party is next week. I can't wait," Danielle said, smacking gum from her end of the phone.

With all of the excitement, I had forgotten about my birthday party. I had nothing to wear. "Did y'all give out all of the invitations?" I asked.

They both assured me that they had. It was good to know that my BFFs were on top of their jobs even when I neglected mine.

Danielle cleared her throat a few times. "I don't mean to rain on your parade, but I think it needs to be said."

I was polishing my fingernails as we talked. "Say it."

"I wouldn't trust Jasmine if I were you."

"She's not going to do anything to bring a negative light to our family. She doesn't want to upset Dion."

"She had no problems leaking to them that you were Dion's child. Just please don't trust her," Danielle urged me.

"Danielle, you're not jealous, are you?" I asked. I polished my pinky nail and then closed the top.

"Of Jasmine? Please. I just don't want you to get hurt," she assured me.

"Tara, you're awfully quiet. What do you have to say about the situation?" I asked her.

"Nothing. That's your sister, so I'm staying out of it."

"Coward," Danielle said.

"Jasmine might change," Tara said.

"I doubt it," Danielle responded.

My phone beeped. "Speaking of Jasmine, that's her now. I'll talk to y'all later."

"See? It's started already. You're pushing your friends aside for her," Danielle stated.

"Whatever, Dani. I'll talk to y'all later." I clicked over to my other line.

"I begged and cried, and Dad finally agreed to let me do the show," Jasmine said. "He knows how important this is for me. I want to be an actress, and this could be my golden shot."

"While you're going that angle, I've decided to use the show as a catalyst for my music career. I've had hopes of being a singer one day," I told her.

"Really? I didn't know you sing."

"Girl, me and my BFFs have our own little group called Candy Girlz."

"That's what's up. Then this should work out for both of us. Britney's dad is the super producer Teddy."

"For real? Maybe you can get him to hear us sing on the show then."

Jasmine remained quiet. "I'll check with Britney and see if we can make that happen."

Being on a reality show might work out for me after all, I thought. "Are you coming to my party?"

"Of course. In fact, cameras will be there too filming the whole thing," she said.

"I'm not sure that's a good idea. I need to wait until my dad gets the legal stuff out of the way."

"Oh, they are on the up-and-up. It's the same producers who did the reality show with my family."

"Maybe so, but my dad insists on getting his lawyers to look at the contracts before signing on."

"Well, even if that's in limbo, they'll be filming me, so it still won't be a conflict," Jasmine assured me.

Although I wasn't too keen on the cameras being there for my party, I agreed to allow them. "But make sure they don't get in anyone's way. I want this to be a party nobody forgets."

"Oh, they won't. Trust me," Jasmine said.

Should I trust Jasmine? That was the million-dollar question.

Cole's phone call interrupted my thoughts.

"You're a hard girl to catch up with," he said.

"It's been crazy around here. Sorry, I couldn't make your game."

"No problem. We won. Just wish you could have been there to see me make all those three-pointers."

"I'm sure you represented our school well."

"You know I did." Cole went on and on about the game.

"So what did you do after the game?" I asked.

"Went home to bed, since you weren't available to hang out."

"You know I'm dealing with some family issues right now."

"Everybody's talking about it too. I've been trying to tell them to mind their own business when someone steps to me with it."

"Thanks for having my back, boo."

"You know I do."

"That's what's up," I responded.

"You're my baby, and I'll do anything for you."

"You're making me blush, Cole."

"Can I come over tomorrow?" he asked.

"Hmm. I don't know. I'll have to ask my parents," I said.

"Next week is your party. I just wanted to meet your father before then."

"I'm thinking it might be best to wait until next week."

I liked Cole. In fact, I thought I even loved Cole, but with all the stuff going on around here, I wasn't too sure if meeting my parents right now was a good idea.

"I'm sure they'll like me," he said. "They just have to get to know me."

I agreed. Cole was a likeable type of guy. That's one of the reasons why I was beginning to think I loved him.

~ 38 ~

People who normally didn't talk to me were all in my face the following week at school. Those who didn't have an invitation to my party were trying to secure one through me or one of my BFFs. They were disappointed when I told them I couldn't invite anyone else. Now if they could get someone to give them their invite and show up in their place, they could. But my mom told me that no more than one hundred people could be invited, and she wasn't budging.

I ran across Brenda, my other sister, one afternoon while waiting for my mom to pick me up. She was running late due to a traffic accident.

"Has Jas been giving you any problems?" Brenda asked.

"We're cool," I responded.

"What do you want for your birthday?" she asked.

"I want a car, but I don't have my license yet, so I don't know if that's going to happen."

"I got this for my sixteenth birthday, but now it's time for an upgrade." Brenda was pointing to her convertible Mustang with caramel leather seats.

"I love it," I said.

"One day, I'll come pick you up and take you for a ride."

Before Brenda and I could continue talking, Jasmine and her friends walked up. "Porsha, you know Britney and Sierra, don't you?" Jasmine asked.

We exchanged greetings. "Well, there goes my mom. I'll see y'all later," I said, as I walked toward where my mom was driving.

"See you're getting all chummy with your sisters," my mom said, as I got in the car.

"Just speaking. Nothing more," I told her.

"If you are, there's nothing wrong with it. I want you to be close to your sisters."

"I'm still trying to figure Jasmine out. She's being cordial when she sees me, but we really haven't talked much since I agreed to do the reality show."

"It's going to take one day at a time. At least you two aren't going at it anymore."

Mom had a point. We were now civil with one another. We both had our own personal agendas for doing the reality show, but I had one thing on Jasmine. I knew she leaked the information, and she didn't want Dion to know about it. I hadn't shared that tidbit with anyone.

Mom surprised me by stopping by the mall before going home. We spent the afternoon buying several outfits for my party. I got a cute pink cowboy hat with matching pink cowboy boots and shirt to match.

"I have a surprise for you. My personal designer will have your dress designed for your formal wear."

"Gwen Beloti's the best," I said. I couldn't hold my excitement. I would be the envy of all my friends if I wore one of her creations.

"It should be waiting for us when we get home," Mom said.

And, sure enough, there was a package with my name on it waiting for me in the foyer. We went to my room, and my mom helped me take it from the box. My mouth hung in awe when I removed the deep purple dress from the garment bag. The fabric felt heavenly.

I stepped out of my clothes and tried the dress on. *Perfect*. The knee-length dress was classy, yet youthful. The shimmer on top matched my widened smile.

"Magnificent. A dress for a princess," Mom said.

I twirled around in my dress and didn't want to take it off. "I can't wait until Saturday," I said, when I finally forced myself to carefully get out of the dress.

My mom helped me put it back on its hanger, and she placed it in my closet for me, while I changed into some other clothes.

"My baby's growing up," she said, teary-eyed when she exited the closet.

"I'll always be your baby," I assured her. "So, is that my birthday present from you?" I asked.

"That's one of them."

"What else did you get me?"

"You'll have to wait and see."

"Please, just one hint."

"The party is part of it."

"Duh. Besides that."

"Girl, do your homework. Dinner will be ready in about two hours," she said, leaving me alone with my thoughts.

My folks could afford a cook, but my mom did most of the cooking. She did have a maid come in and clean the house a couple of times a week, but for the most part, the amount of money we had didn't stop her from doing everyday chores.

I had to go to my parents' room to use my laptop to work on my school assignments.

My dad entered while I was finishing up my social studies assignment. "Ready for your big day?" he asked.

"I am, now that I got my outfits together."

"Well, dear, I was going to wait until Saturday to give it to you, but I heard you got this new designer dress, and every designer dress should have this."

He brought forth a pink floral bag and placed it in front of me. I unwrapped the box inside and, to my amazement, it was a diamond necklace with teardrop earrings to match. I needed sunglasses to shade my eyes from the sparkles. *It would be perfect with my new designer dress.*

"A girl only turns sixteen once, and I wanted you to have this as something to remember this time by."

"Dad, you're the greatest." I hugged his neck tight. I really meant it too. Trey was the best dad a girl could ever ask for. If I'm getting these early gifts, I wondered what was in store for my actual birthday. I wanted the week to rush on by.

~ 39 ~

Cole had been sticking to me closer than glue the remainder of the week. He walked me to class every chance he got and made sure we sat with each other for lunch. I could tell Danielle and Tara were feeling a little jealous about our closeness, from some of the snide comments they made. Eric would be at the table too, but I couldn't tell which one of my friends he really liked because he would laugh and joke with both of them.

Friday had come, and Cole had a game. I wouldn't be attending because I had too much stuff to do before my party the following day. My mom was having Dawn, her personal hairdresser, come out to the house to do my hair, Danielle's, and Tara's.

Jasmine ran up to us while we were leaving the building to go meet my mom. "Do you need me to be there early tomorrow?" she asked.

"Just whenever. The invite says four. So four is fine," I responded.

"Don't forget the camera crew will be there," she added.

"I told my mom. She wasn't too happy about it, but it's cool."

"Dad wasn't too happy about it either. He'll get over it," Jasmine said.

I saw my mom waving, trying to get our attention. "We got to go. See you tomorrow," I said.

"Tell your mom I said hi," Jasmine said, as we were walking away.

"I still don't trust her," Danielle said.

I didn't respond. Once inside the car, I delivered Jasmine's message to my mom.

"She's trying," my mom commented.

"I guess." I shrugged.

"So you girls ready to get *glam-o-fied*?" my mom said.

Danielle pulled out several tubes of lip gloss. "I got my lip gloss, my eye shadow. I'm ready."

"Tonight, we're just doing the hair. Tomorrow, I'll have my makeup artist do all of your makeup. I want it to look natural."

"Dani's real good with makeup," I said.

"Really? Well, that's good. You girls are growing up, and I know you want to look glam for the boys. Speaking of which, I'll finally get to spend a little time getting to know Cole better."

I began to look out the window. I was hoping she didn't embarrass me by talking about Cole, but no such luck.

"What do you girls think about Cole?" Mom asked.

Tara responded first. "I think he's cool."

"He's nice. He really likes Porsha."

Mom asked them, "So, would you date him?"

"Mom!"

"Well, would you?"

Danielle said, "If Porsha didn't like him, yes, I would."

Tara said, "No, because I don't date ballers."

"When you realize how much ballers make, you'll change your mind," my mom joked.

We all laughed.

"Ms. Angela, that's what I keep trying to tell her," Danielle said.

My phone beeped with a text message. It was Cole telling me he missed me. I sent him a quick text back saying the same.

"Who was that?" Mom asked.

"Probably Cole," Danielle teased.

"Whatever." I rolled my eyes. "Don't hate."

"So, girls, are you bringing a date to the party tomorrow?"

Danielle responded, "In fact, I'll be bringing Eric."

Stop the presses. This was the first I'd heard of this. I loosened my seatbelt and turned around so I could face Danielle. "Wow! And you hadn't told your best friend? I'm hurt."

"I just asked him today. He said yes. I was going to tell you."

"So, Tara, who are you bringing?" I asked.

"Eric said he has a friend that's interested in me, so it'll be a blind date."

My mom commented, "I've never liked going out on blind dates. They never worked out for me. It was always something funny or unusual about the guy."

"Mom, that was then."

"Tara, just don't get your hopes high on this blind date. If he start tripping, you come get me or Trey, and we'll put him out of the party."

"Yes, ma'am."

I rolled my eyes and turned back around in my seat.

Later on that evening we laughed and joked while Dawn did our hair. We felt like celebrities, with her and her assistants working their magic. I was wearing my hair up so that my mom could put my tiara on my head when it was time for me to dress in my new designer gown for the following night.

Danielle's mom stopped by around nine to pick her and Tara up to take them home.

I was riding on a natural high, so it was hard for me to go to sleep. Although the gossip on the Internet still wasn't favorable about Mom and Dion, it wasn't bothering me. In less than two hours, I would be sixteen. I had a boyfriend who adored me, and soon fans that would too, with the onset of the reality show. Life for me was more than good.

I dozed off, but my phone ringing woke me up. "Hello," I said sluggishly.

"Happy birthday," Cole's voice rang from the other end.

I turned over and glanced at the clock, eyes squinted. It was one minute after midnight. "Thank you," I managed to say.

"I wanted to be the first one to wish you happy birthday. I wanted you to know I care about you a whole lot and thank you for being my girl."

"Aw, how sweet. I'm glad you're my man."

"I hope you like the gift I got you," he said.

"I know I'll like anything coming from you."

"Goodnight, my princess," were the last words I heard before drifting back to sleep.

~ 40 ~

"Happy birthday, sleepyhead," my mom said, as she peeked her head inside my bedroom.

Followed behind her were Jay, Jason, and Dad. They were holding a plate of pancakes with a birthday candle on top.

I sat up in bed and rubbed my eyes. "Thank you all. I feel so special."

"You are special, dear," Dad said.

Jason and Jay ran and hugged me. "Happy birthday, big sis."

Jay said, "We want you to know you'll always be our sister, no matter what."

"Aw, that's so sweet." I hugged them both tight.

"Boys, stop," my dad said. "Here you are. Now make a wish." He handed me the plate of pancakes and then lit the candle.

I took a deep breath, closed my eyes, and blew the candle out.

"What did you wish for?" Jason asked.

"I have everything I need right here, so my wish already came true," I responded.

My mom wiped her teary eyes. "Boys, you go get dressed. We have a full day ahead," she said, in an attempt to get rid of them.

"I'm going to make sure they do that," Dad said, leaving us in the room together.

I got up and placed the plate on my desk. I knew this was a special day because normally we weren't allowed to eat food in our rooms, so bringing me my favorite, blueberry pancakes, to my room was a great way to start off my birthday.

My mom slipped something out of her pocket and handed it to me. It was an envelope. "I thought you would need this."

I retrieved the contents of the envelope and saw a check for one hundred thousand dollars. My mouth flew open. It was signed by the producer of the show. "So this means I can do it?"

"Yes, we signed the deal. They overnighted the check, and we got it yesterday. I just decided to wait until today to present it to you."

"Happy birthday to me." I kept my eye glued on the check, my very first paycheck, and it was six figures.

"Hold off on some of the excitement. You will be getting monthly allotments, but most of the money will be put away in a trust fund," Mom said.

I pouted. "But, Mom—"

"But Mom, nothing. As your parent, I have to look out for our future." She paused and continued to say, "Also fifteen percent will be going to your manager."

"What manager?" I asked.

She took the check back from me. "Me. I'm going to be your manager and make sure nobody tries to mistreat my baby."

"But, Mom, with your jewelry line you're promoting, you're not going to have time."

"I'll just put it on hold for now."

"No, Mom, I don't want you to do that for me. You've worked too hard. Why not have Leslie recommend someone?" I really didn't think me and my mom would work well, so that's one reason why I wanted her to find me another manager.

"I'll ask around. But, in the meantime, until we can get you someone official, I'm it. Deal?"

I paused. I stared. I responded, "Deal."

We shook hands on it. I was hoping she could find me someone soon. Our personalities clashed, and how would it look if she made me mad and I had to fire my own mother? I shook my head. That wouldn't be a good look at all.

Now on to more pressing things, like figuring out what I was going to put on before my shindig later on. I opted to wear one of the new outfits my mom had bought me earlier in the week. Purple was one of my favorite colors, so I adorned myself in purple from head to toe, even to the flavor of lip gloss I wore, the grape delight lip gloss rounding off my look.

When I finally made it downstairs, I was surprised to see that it had been decorated in pink and purple balloons. Yes, it was my birthday, and I was enjoying every minute of it. My cell phone rang in my pocket. Dion's number flashed across the screen. I eagerly answered it.

"Happy birthday, Porsha," he said.

"Thanks, Dion."

"So, are you ready for your party?" he asked.

"Yes. I can't wait until four."

"I'll be there. I'm sending a limousine to pick up you and your friends. What time do you want it to be there?"

"Really? Oh, man, that'll be cool. Hold on. Let me check." I hit the mute button and went to locate my mom. "Mom, what time should Dion send the limo to pick us up?"

"Limo, huh? Well, tell him they need to be here no later than two o'clock. You need to be there a little early, so you can make a grand entrance on the white stallion your dad hired just for you."

My day kept getting better and better. I removed the mute button. "She said two o'clock. I also just found out I'm riding in on a white stallion for my birthday. I can't wait to ride her."

"It'll be there. Have fun. I'll see you later to give you your other gift," he responded.

I was in a jovial mood. By lunch time, Danielle and Tara were here. My mom served us some hors d'œuvres, but I was too nervous and excited to eat anything solid.

After we ate and chatted, my mom's makeup artist and assistants did our faces. We admired each other and felt like the little princesses we were.

We changed into our outfits for the first portion of my party. I wore my blue jeans and my pink shirt with the tassels. I stood up and modeled my pink Stetson cowboy boots.

Danielle said, "I want those boots."

"Fierce. I know."

"How you like these?" Tara said, as she removed her red boots from her bag.

"Aw! No, you ain't trying to outdo the birthday girl," I said. "I love those."

"Well, you know I had to go with the purple to match my shirt." Danielle pulled hers out.

"Ladies, we're hot. That's all I have to say," I said.

"Yes, we are," Danielle and Tara said in unison.

~ 41 ~

"Girls, it's time," my mom stuck her head in my room and said.

"How are we going to fit all of this in the car?" Danielle asked.

"Surprise. Dion's hired us a limo. We're riding to the party in a limo, ladies," I informed them.

"Cool."

My mom said, "Grab your garment bags and come on."

It took us about thirty minutes to get everything situated with my clothes and their clothes, and I wanted to make sure I didn't forget anything.

Before I got in the limousine, my mom said, "We'll be right behind you. If you get there before we do, don't misbehave."

"Mom, I know how to act."

"Just saying."

"We'll hold the noise down, I promise." I hugged her and entered the limousine. I poured us each a

glass of sparkling water in champagne glasses.
"Happy birthday to me, happy birthday," I sang.

All of our cell phones were vibrating with text messages about my party today. I had received happy birthday greetings from people I didn't even know knew me.

Danielle said, "Your party is the talk of the school. People who didn't get invites are jealous of those who did."

"That's what's up," I said with a smile on my face.

The staff at Southfork Ranch welcomed us with open arms. We were led to what was to be my room while there for the night. The limousine driver and helpers my folks had hired got our stuff out of the limousine, so we didn't have to lift a finger.

My parents and little brothers showed up shortly thereafter.

"Everything looks great," my dad said.

"Yes. Perfect." My mom looked at me. "What do you think?"

"Yes. Decorated just nice, Mom. I love it." I gave her a tight hug. "Now where's the horse I'll be riding?" I asked. I had been trying to hold back my excitement, but now that they were here, I couldn't wait to see it and ride it.

"Ladies, follow me," my dad said.

We followed his command and were led out back to the ranch area. As we walked, I noticed how things were decorated. *All of this for me?* I felt so special. I had to be the luckiest girl alive.

We reached the stables, and the whitest and shiniest horse stood in front of us.

I rushed ahead of everybody, so I could get a closer look. I reached over and began to rub my hand on his side. His coat felt like silk. "Hi, cutie. What's your name? You're so pretty."

My dad responded, "His name is Snowflake."

"He's beautiful," Tara said, once they reached where I stood.

"I love him," Danielle added.

My dad opened up the stable door. "You want to ride him now, or wait?"

I looked at my mom and back at him. "I want to test him out now."

"Let me saddle him up," he said.

After he placed the saddle on Snowflake, he helped me up. It was a perfect fit. It had been a little while since I rode a horse, so it took me a minute to get comfortable. But once I did, I felt comfortable taking Snowflake for a ride outside the stable.

"Be careful," my mom said.

My dad got on one of the other horses in the stable. "We'll be back shortly. You girls find you a horse you want to ride later."

My dad and I took our two horses for a short ride. Snowflake was made for me as he seemed to glide as we rode. We were on the other side of the ranch by now.

"So how do you like him?" my dad asked.

"I love him. I can't thank you enough," I responded. I slid off Snowflake. I rubbed his face.

"You're growing up so fast. Next thing I know, you'll be going away to college."

Do I see a tear in his eye? I think I do. I couldn't believe my dad was about to get so emotional on me. I didn't know how to react to that, so I said, "I'll always be your little girl, remember?"

"Yes, but so much has changed. You mean so much to me, Porsha. You're my daughter in every sense of the word."

"I know," I assured him. We hadn't really talked since I had been spending time with Dion and talking to him. "Dion is my father, but he's no substitute for you."

"I wasn't worried about that."

"He's not as bad as I thought he was. I have to give him credit. Once he realized I was his daughter, he's been trying to establish a relationship. I haven't made it easy, but it doesn't stop him."

"He could do better," my dad responded. "It's hard watching you grow up and to know that I'm having to share you."

"I have to admit that Dion's cool. He's my dad too, but you've been there for me since birth. I wouldn't tell him this, but you'll always be my favorite dad if I had to choose one. I doubt there would be many men who would have raised up a daughter they knew wasn't theirs. You did, and I never felt like I was unwanted."

"Come here." He grabbed me and hugged me tight. "I love you."

"I love you too, Dad. Now stop this before you ruin my makeup." I tried to lighten up the situation as I wiped the tears from my face.

"Come on, let's get back to the ranch before your mom sends out a search party."

"You know she would."

He helped me back on my saddle, and we raced back to the stables, where my mother and BFFs were standing around waiting for us.

"Did y'all have a nice ride?" my mom asked.

"Perfect," I said, as I looked at my dad and winked my right eye.

~ 42 ~

"Showtime! Your guests have arrived," my mom said.

We were now freshening up and had discussed our grand entrance.

"How's my hat?" I asked.

My mom adjusted it. "Perfect. Now you girls go get on your horses, so you can make your grand entrance. Your dad will do the announcement."

Jasmine's voice could be heard outside of my room. "I'm her sister. She won't mind me coming in."

My mom turned. "What in the world? Let me straighten this out." She turned to the worker. "I told you no one was to come back here."

The timid woman responded, "She told me she was her sister."

Jasmine walked up from behind with two men holding video cameras. "I didn't know I had to wait with everyone else."

My mom blocked her from entering the room. "Dear, you and those cameras"—She pointed to the men behind her—"will have to wait outside like everybody else."

"But it's my sister's birthday, and I wanted to give her an early present," Jasmine pled.

"That's fine, Mom," I said. "I'll talk to her."

"Five minutes. That's all the time you have. Come on, Danielle and Tara."

They remained standing, not wanting to miss anything.

"Come on, ladies," Mom said, and this time they obeyed.

Jasmine and I were now alone, well, almost alone, since one of the cameramen was standing behind her.

She surprised me by reaching out to hug me. "Happy birthday, sis."

"Thanks," I said, as I readjusted my hat.

She reached into her small handbag and gave me a little gift box. "This is just something I wanted you to have."

I opened the Tiffany box and retrieved a charm bracelet filled with several charms, including musical instruments. One charm stood out. It read, "My sister."

"Aw, thank you, Jasmine." I wasn't sure what to do with my newfound emotions. To break the silence between us, I said, "Well, I better get out there before my mom comes back looking for me."

"Sure. It's your day. I didn't want to hold you up, I just wanted you to have this."

"Before I go, can you help me put it on?"

She snapped on the bracelet. "Looks good."

"Thanks again." I hugged her.

After our sister moment, I went to meet up with my mom and friends. They were already mounted on their horses when I got to the stables.

"What took you so long?" my mom asked.

"She just wanted me to have this." I hung out my arm, so she could see the charm bracelet dangling from my wrist.

She looked at it. "Nice. Now get up there, because your dad's ready to announce you."

Snowflake looked different. She was now adorned with a pink shawl over her with my name on it. She was ready to escort the birthday princess to the party.

I rubbed her head. "Ready, Snowflake? Show-time."

Tara and Danielle went outside, and I could hear the cheers.

My dad announced, "Now, the belle of the party, my daughter, Ms. Sweet Sixteen, Porsha Swint."

Everyone cheered as I made my grand entrance. I waved my hand as if I was Miss America. Snowflake seemed to enjoy being the center of attention too, strutting, leading us to the front of the podium, where my dad stood.

I scanned the crowd hoping to see Cole. He caught my attention as he waved frantically. I blew him a kiss.

Standing near my dad when I reached the podium was my second family: Dion, Brenda, Jasmine and Kim, who I was surprised to see there.

My dad helped me off Snowflake, and one of the workers went to tie her up. I was led up the steps to stand behind the microphone. I hadn't practiced a speech, so I was a little nervous.

My dad whispered in my ear, "Take a few deep breaths. Just say what's on your heart."

I did as was told. "Thank you all for coming to share this special day with me. Because of you all being here, I can already say this is my best birthday ever. It couldn't have happened without my two wonderful parents, who I love dearly. Thanks, Mom and Dad."

The crowd cheered.

I continued when the noise died down some, "Well, I don't have much to say, but thank you for coming and let's have some fun."

Cole made his way to the front and gave me a hug.

"Dad."

Both Dion and my dad looked in my direction.

"I want you all to meet Cole, the guy I've been telling you about."

They all shook hands.

My mom said, "I'm glad to see you again."

"Same here," he responded.

"I understand you're a fan of mine," my dad said proudly.

"Yes, sir. I know all of your stats by heart."

Dion interjected, "I understand you play basketball. Any reason why you didn't play football?"

"I found out I was better at basketball, so I decided to concentrate in that area."

My dad said, "Well, son, with either sport, it requires discipline and dedication. Never forget where you came from."

My mom cleared her throat. "I hate to interrupt this man fest, but it's my baby girl's day, so can we hold off talking about sports for once?"

"Thanks, Mom. Yes, I agree," I said, with a smile on my face. I was happy that my dads were bonding with my boyfriend. But, like my mom said, this was my day, so their bonding session needed to be put on hold.

It was time to get the party started. My mouth dropped opened when I saw, coming to the stage to get it crunked, no other than my favorite rapper, Soulja Boy.

"I understand it's somebody's birthday," he said as he took the stage.

I was too excited to speak.

Dion said, "I hope you're not disappointed."

"Thank you." I gave him a tight hug.

"Porsha, this song's for you," Soulja Boy said. When he burst out the lyrics to his latest song, me and my BFFs sang and danced along.

~ 43 ~

The crowd was dancing along to all of the Soulja Boy songs.

Cole held me up as I almost tripped. "I think I'm going to sit this next one out," I said.

He followed behind me as we headed to the table that had cold drinks. "I'll take a water," I told the server. Cole took the bottle, opened it, and handed it to me. I gulped down the water fast.

Jasmine seemed to come from out of nowhere. "Looks like you're having fun," she said.

"Aren't you? This party is crunked," Cole said.

"I wasn't talking to you," Jasmine said.

Oh, no. Now this was the Jasmine we all knew and hated. "Chill out. He was just making an observation."

"Look, we got some good footage so far. Do you have anything you want to say for the cameras?" she asked.

The cameras were on me. "Yes. I want to say that turning sixteen is a milestone in any girl's life. Being able to share it with family and friends is a blessing. I feel like I'm one lucky girl. Plus, I'm with the hottest guy at Plano High. What more can a girl ask for?" I looped my arm through Cole's.

Jasmine's smile faded away with that gesture. "Well, we're going to get some more footage. I'll see you around." She stormed away.

Cole whispered in my ear, "I don't think your sister likes me anymore."

"And that's a bad thing?" I asked.

"It's great. I was trying not to hurt her feelings."

I saw a flash, turned around, and saw one of the cameramen was still there. He gave me a thumbs-up signal.

Oops. He got everything we said on film. I didn't think Jasmine was going to be too happy about what we had to say. Oh, well. It was her idea to bring the cameras.

"Ooh, that's my song." I grabbed Cole's hand and led him back on stage.

We danced and cheered as my friends all got crunked.

I yelled, "It's my birthday! Let's do this! It's my birthday!"

After Soulja Boy's performance, it was time for some competitive games where people could win prizes. My dad went way out. I found him and Dion holding a civil conversation.

"Baby girl, are you having fun?" he asked.

"You know it. I can't thank you and Mom enough for this. It's different, and everybody seems to be having a great time."

"As long as you're happy, I'm happy," he said, as he hugged me.

"Where's your boyfriend?" Dion asked.

I looked around. "He's around here somewhere. Probably stuffing his face with some barbecue."

"The food is good, Trey. I have to hand it to you. You've pulled off a great event," Dion commented.

"Anything for my baby girl," he responded.

"Dad," I said.

Both of them looked at me.

I was talking to Trey and didn't mean to hurt Dion's feelings. "Let me get back to my guests." I left them alone talking and went in search of Danielle and Tara. I caught them in a heated conversation.

"Tell Eric his friend is a jerk," Tara said. "I do not want anything to do with him."

"What happened?" I asked, as I walked up to them near the house.

"Do you know he's been all up in Jasmine's face the whole time?" Tara stated.

"Man, that's messed up," I said.

"I told Eric he was wrong."

I felt sorry that Tara's date acted like a jerk. "If you want me to, I can kick him out," I said.

"No, that would be too embarrassing. Just keep him as far away from me as possible." Tara stormed away.

Danielle said, "I'm sorry it didn't work out for her, but she didn't have to jump on me about it."

"Tell me this. Did Jasmine start making passes at him?" I asked.

"I really don't know. Tara brought it to my attention."

"I'll get to the bottom of this. Eric brought the guy for Tara, so he should have been concentrating on her, not some other chick."

"Even if that other chick happens to be your sister?" Danielle asked.

I ignored her question and went in search of Jasmine. I saw her and some boy, who I supposed was Eric's friend. "Jas, can I talk to you for a minute?" I interrupted without bothering to introduce myself.

"Sure. Braylon, I'll be right back."

Jasmine followed me away from the crowd. "What's up?" she asked.

"Braylon, or whatever his name is, was supposed to be Tara's date, but from what I understand, you're up in each other's faces." I stood with my hands crossed.

"I've had my eye on Braylon for a while. When I saw him at your party, he let me know he had been feeling me too. I didn't know he was here for your friend Tara. Besides, why are you worried about who Tara is with? You got your man."

"Look, I don't like drama. This is my party, and what Braylon did wasn't right. The fact that you're participating in it doesn't sit well with me."

"Again, I didn't know Braylon was here for your girl."

"Well, now that you know, back up off him."

"I'm sorry I can't do that. Braylon pursued me. I didn't pursue him. Tara needs to get over it and find her own man."

As much as I hated to admit it, Jasmine was right. Tara didn't need to be with a guy if he wasn't feeling her like that. "Okay, to cut down on confusion, please just stay out of Tara's way. Can you do that for me?"

Jasmine smiled. "Anything for you, sis."

"Good. Now I got more people to see. Enjoy the rest of the party," I said, as I left Jasmine alone with the cameraman.

~ 44 ~

My mom gathered up me, Danielle, and Tara so we could get ready for the second part of my party. We took turns showering. My curls had fallen a little, so my mom re-did my hair. And Danielle re-applied our makeup because we had sweated it out in that Texas heat.

"You girls make me proud," my mom said as she admired our final output. She grabbed her camera and took our pictures. "We've rolled out the red carpet. You'll all stop and pose for the photographers. I want different shots but, of course, I had to take my own."

"Dani and Tara, I'll be out in a minute. I want to talk to my mom alone for a minute," I said.

"What's wrong, baby?" she asked.

"Nothing. I just wanted to apologize for my behavior these past few weeks," I said.

She reached for my hand. "No apology necessary. It's been intense in the Swint household.

I take full blame for it all. You didn't ask for the changes. I should have told you and Dion sooner."

"Like you tell me, that's water under the bridge now."

"My little girl is acting all grown up on me." She gave me a tight hug. "Now come on. It's time for the queen and her princess to make their grand entrance into the ball."

We walked out of the room hand in hand.

"I hope Cole is waiting nearby."

"He's been instructed not to move. I got your brothers on that."

"Oh no, Cole's going to jet for real. They are going to run him away."

We both laughed.

I felt like a superstar as I we glided out of the room and down the red carpet. We stopped and took pictures. I took pictures with both of my BFFs, my two dads, my mom and brothers, Cole, and then, finally, by myself.

Everyone marveled at how beautiful I looked in my designer dress, and the necklace my dad gave me accented it perfectly. My three-inch heels sparkled as I walked. An announcement was made when I entered the ballroom area.

Everyone stopped and looked in my direction as Cole escorted me in. He led me to the front of the room, and I took a seat at the front table adorned with pink and purple flowers. I noticed each table had a glass-slipper drink fountain filled with never-ending pink punch.

"Wow! Your parents went way out," Cole whispered as he held my chair for me to sit down.

"Looks good," I agreed.

Danielle sat next to Eric. Tara sat in between me and Danielle. I noticed Jasmine had Tara's date sitting next to her.

"Why does she keep looking down this way?" Tara asked.

"Chill out. Ignore them. This is my party. Don't even think about them."

"I can't help it. It's like she's eating up every word he says."

"He's a jerk anyway. Forget him," I said.

"Ladies, I can hear you all the way over here, so I know they can." My mom's eyes darted to the end of the table, where Jasmine sat with Tara's supposed-to-be date.

I rolled my eyes because I didn't care. Jasmine didn't have to sit him at our table.

Tara whispered, "I know she's your sister, but I can't stand her."

"Shh," I said. "Just ignore them."

"I'll try."

Waiters came and served our food. I didn't think anyone would be hungry after all the barbecue consumed, but I was wrong. Soon, all you heard was the tinkling of silverware hitting the fine china dishes.

"This food is scrumptious," my mom said from across the table.

After dinner, my dad said, "We're going to move this event to one of the other ballrooms. Dion has a surprise for you."

"Really?" I was surprised that he and Dion were getting along so well. In fact, real surprised that he would even let him participate in the party that he put so much energy into. I was loving him even more. His selfless acts were amazing. I vowed then that my future husband would have to have all of the qualities of Trey Swint.

I was anticipating the surprise Dion had for me. People started heading toward to the ballroom. I was led up front, with Cole and my two BFFs on my heels.

Dion had the microphone. "I know by now everyone has heard that Porsha is my daughter. I wanted to tell her how proud of her I am, and I appreciate Trey and Angie for allowing me to spend this special night with her." He looked at my dad and mom, who both had smiles on their faces.

I looked over at Jasmine. Her face showed a half-smile, but it couldn't mask her body language that indicated she wasn't happy about his words. I turned my attention back to Dion.

"I asked her dad who one of her favorite artists was, besides Soulja Boy, and he told me. So, thanks to Teddy, who's a good friend of mine, I was able to get the following guest to come and sing happy birthday while we get ready to cut the cake, and then you all can party."

"Who?" I yelled out. The excitement was killing me.

The lights dimmed. I heard the words sung, *"Happy birthday to Porsha,"* and the lights came back on, with the spotlight on no other than Trey Songz.

Cole had to hold me because I almost passed out. "Oh my God!" I yelled out. "That's Trey Songz!" I could barely breathe.

"Calm down, baby," Cole said. He grabbed my hand and led me up to my four-tier birthday cake with a pink slipper on the top.

By the time Trey finished singing "Happy Birthday" to me, I was floating on cloud nine. He topped it off by kissing me on the cheek.

"This is a dream come true." My hand flew to my cheek. *I'm never washing this cheek again.*

"I heard it was your birthday, and I wanted to make sure you had a good one." He winked his eye.

"Thank you so much."

"Anything for you. Now let me get back to doing what I was paid to do." He grabbed the microphone and sang some of his hits, and Cole and I, along with all the guests, rocked along to the songs.

~ 45 ~

After the mini-concert my favorite singer put on, I didn't think my night could get any better. My mom announced, "It's now time for the gifts."

There was no way I would be able to open all of the many gifts. After opening up a few and realizing how much time it was taking and also seeing how overwhelmed I looked, my mom got on the microphone and said, "Porsha will finish opening up her gifts later. She will be thanking each of you personally, either in person, phone call, or handwritten note."

My dad walked up to me and handed me a gift bag. "This is from your mother and I." He kissed me on the cheek.

The room got quiet. I removed the box. It was an all-expense paid trip for four, which meant I could take my two BFFs along with me to the Bahamas. "Thank you so much," I said, as I hugged them both. "Girls, we're going to the Bahamas."

"I'm so jealous," Brenda said from behind me.

"I have an open ticket, so you can go too."

"I better go, because I'm sure you're going to need a chaperone." She winked her eye.

Me and my older sister were going to be all right.

My dad went on to say. "Dion and I were talking, and we both decided that we would put our differences aside and join together and get you what any sixteen-year-old would want."

"Close your eyes," Dion said.

I did as I was told as they led me out the door. Dion was on one side of me, and my dad was on the other. I could feel the cool breeze sweeping under my dress.

I heard "Oohs," and "Ahhs."

"Okay, open up," my dad said.

"Oh my God!" My hand flew up to my mouth. Standing before me was a black BMW 650i convertible.

"Here's the keys," my dad said.

I snatched them from him and jumped in the driver's seat. My two BFFs rushed to the other side.

My mom said, "Now, you don't have your license yet, so we can't let you drive it home, but those two insisted that we present it to you tonight." She looked over at Dion and my dad.

Both looked like two proud fathers.

I cranked it up and turned to my favorite Dallas radio station K104 and let the music blast as those around us started singing along and cheering me along.

"Happy birthday to me!" I yelled out.

After the excitement died down, I turned the engine off and exited the car. "Thank you, Daddy," I said out loud as I approached Dion and my dad.

Both men looked in my direction. I hugged my dad first. He acted like he didn't want to release me, but soon did. I paused for a minute and hugged Dion. "Thanks, Dad," I said in his ear.

I saw a tear in his eye. He said, "Do you realize what you just did?"

"What?"

"You called me Dad for the first time. I'll never forget this day." Dion wiped his eye and then walked away.

I looked at Trey.

He said, "That's okay. He is your dad too. So if you want to call him Dad, I'm okay with it."

Relief swept across my face. *Two dads and a mom who love me.* I was one lucky girl, or as my grandmother from Shreveport, Louisiana would say, I was one blessed girl. *I wish she was alive to see me, but I know she is looking down from heaven above.* I looked up into the sky, and as if on cue, I saw the sparkle of one lonely star.

Cole walked up to me and pulled me away from my dad. "I can't wait for you to allow me to take a spin in your new wheels," he said.

"Only if you're good," I responded.

Brenda walked up to us. "I guess you no longer will want a ride in my convertible Mustang."

I laughed. "You still owe me a ride."

"Only if you let me drive that baby."

"Ain't nobody driving that baby until I do," I said.

"It's all right. I want me a Jaguar. Those are better cars."

Brenda said, "Stop hating, Jasmine. You were drooling over that car when you saw it."

"Was not." She pouted.

"Yes, you were."

"Brenda, leave your sister alone," Kim said.

I hadn't realized she was there until I heard her open her mouth. "Kim, thanks for coming," I said.

"We're family now . . . extended family, but family nevertheless," she said, sounding a little slurred.

"Mom, have you been drinking?" Brenda left my side to go stand nearer to Kim.

"I'm a grown woman," she snapped. "I don't answer to you, my child."

"Uh-oh. Sounds like some drama brewing," Cole said.

"Yes, and I'm out of here. I got enough drama to deal without having to worry about theirs," I responded.

Cole and I made our exit as the McNeils dealt with their own issues. Cole whisked me away to a vacant room. "Finally, I get the birthday girl all to herself," he said, as he embraced me.

His cologne filled my nostrils, making me dizzy. Before I could react, his lips were on top of mine. This was only the second time we had shared a kiss. His soft lips caused me to lose my balance as my hormones went out of whack. I knew I had to pull back. This wasn't the time, nor the place for us to be caught kissing. The feelings I felt were foreign to me. I had to get a grip on them.

I pulled back. "Cole, we should stop."

"Baby, it's nobody here but you and me. We're only kissing."

"Yes, but what if my folks walk in?" I was trying to think rationally in an irrational situation. "And is that alcohol I smell on your breath?"

Cole blew his breath in his hand. "Oh, that's nothing. I just took a sip of a beer Braylon had earlier."

"Are you serious? There's not supposed to be any liquor. If my folks find out, they are going to kill me."

"Calm down, Porsha. The beer's in the car. We know not to bring it out for anyone to see."

"But still. I didn't even know you drink."

"I don't drink often. Every now and then. Besides, a few beers won't hurt."

"Well, put a mint in your mouth or something, because your breath stinks."

Cole did as I told him. "Is that better?"

"Yes, but still don't think we're going to do anything but kiss."

He pulled me into his arms. "Porsha, don't you know by now how much I love you? I would never hurt you."

"Cole, I love you too, but we need to chill, okay. I'm just not ready to go there with you."

"Fine. Another place, another time. Just say you'll think about it," he pled.

I hugged him, trying to figure out how to tell him I vowed to remain a virgin until at least after graduation. I hoped he could wait that long. If not, well, I didn't want to think about that.

~ 46 ~

"We need to get out of here before folks start looking for us." I pulled back and ran my hand down my dress to make sure there weren't any wrinkles.

"So you're just going to blow me off just like that?"

"Cole, where is this hostility coming from? I'm your girl. We have plenty of time for doing those things. Not tonight."

"I'm not talking about tonight. I wouldn't dare disrespect you and your parents like that. I just want to know that, when you do it for the first time, will I be that guy?"

"Yes, of course. But, truthfully, it's going to be a while okay. I've made a mess with my grades these last few months, so my concentration is keeping my grades up so I can go to college."

"My hormones are all over the place. I love you so much, and I want to be with you so bad, I don't know how long I can wait."

Disappointed with his words, I hung my face down. "So what are you saying, Cole?"

"I love you and want to be with you forever, but I have needs. Needs I want my girlfriend to fulfill, not some random chick."

"I can't believe you. Why of all nights are you coming to me with this? Everything was perfect, and you had to ruin it." I pushed past him and out the door.

I heard him yell my name, but I ignored him. I heard Eric ask him, "Man, what's up?"

"I don't know. It's time to blow this joint."

"Let me go get our boy. I'll meet you at the car, and then we can go get some more drinks."

He rushed up behind me. "Porsha, chill, baby. I was just blowing out some steam. Me and my boys, we're going to leave. But this is not over for us. I love you, and we can work it out."

"Not if you insist on having sex, we won't."

"I'll think of another solution."

"You're going to have to," I said.

"Look at me." He twirled me around to face him. "I let my hormones get the best of me back there. I would never cheat on you with another girl."

I rolled my eyes. "Don't think I'm forgiving you this easy."

"Please. I promise to show my patience when it comes to that."

"I'll think about it," I responded.

Eric called out, "Cole!"

"Look. They're ready. Call me when you get home tonight. Love you, okay, pretty girl." He kissed me lightly on the lips.

I didn't say a word until he was out of earshot. "I love you too."

Jasmine clapped her hands. "Aw, did the two lovebirds have a fight?"

"What do you want? Shouldn't you be somewhere dealing with your drunk mama?"

"Keep my mama's name out of your mouth."

"See, I knew it was too good to be true. You're still the same spoiled Jasmine from a few weeks ago."

"You got that right. You think you're something, right. Well, it took two men paying for your car. My dad's going to buy me a car for my birthday all by hisself, and it's going to be bigger and better than a BMW."

"Jasmine, I could care less. Here I thought we were making headway, but now I see you for what Danielle said you were. You haven't changed."

"Danielle's just jealous that you have a sister. I have changed. I was actually starting to like you."

"Liar!" I yelled.

"I was. We're sisters. We're going to have dis-agreements. You see how me and Brenda get along," she stated.

"Y'all don't!"

"Exactly. But I still love her, and us not get-ting along is our way of getting along."

As crazy as it sounded, it made sense coming from her. "Whatever. Just stay out of my way for the rest of the night, please."

"The party's wrapping up anyway. People are leaving."

"Fine. So don't you think you should be fol-lowing suit and leaving too?" I now stood in the middle of the doorway leading back to the party festivities.

"I am, as soon as my mom gets out of the bath-room."

Kim walked up. "There you are. I'm so glad to see you girls getting along."

Jasmine and I both rolled our eyes.

"Dear, I'm glad you had a good birthday. Now don't be speeding in that new car of yours."

"Thanks, Ms. Kim, for coming," I said.

My mom walked up. "She's such a drama queen."

"Like mother. Like daughter," I said.

We both laughed.

"So did you have fun today?" my mom asked, once we both stopped laughing.

"Yes, more fun than anyone should be allowed."

"You only turn sixteen once, and I wanted it to be a day you would never forget."

"Definitely unforgettable. I got to ride a horse, and you guys got me a car. I'm living the life of an urban princess for real." My hands went up in the air.

"Yes, you are. You deserve it, and now you need to concentrate on getting your grades back up," my mom said.

Uh-oh. Busted.

She continued to say, "Progress reports came last week. I wasn't going to say anything until after the party because I know I'm partly to blame. But we're turning over a new leaf now, right?"

"Yes, ma'am."

"Then pull those grades up, and at least make it a strong B."

"I can do that."

"I know you can. Now let me leave and round up some people so we can start packing up some of these gifts."

"I'll go find Dani and Tara," I said.

"No need to. The limousine driver is waiting. He's been instructed to take you straight home.

You girls don't stay up too late now. We'll be home shortly."

I hugged her. "Have I told you you're the greatest?"

"It wouldn't hurt to tell me again," she said, as she hugged me back.

Danielle and Tara were waiting for me by the limousine. The driver opened the door and we got in. I looked out the window at Southfork Ranch and embraced the memories of everything that occurred today as he pulled away.

~ 47 ~

The next morning we were awakened by a knock at the door. "Come in," I said.

Danielle and Tara both stirred. Tara was sleeping on one end of my bed, and Danielle had made a bed on the chaise near my window.

My mom entered. She looked like she had been crying. "Girls, I need to talk to you before you hear it from anyone else."

I shot up in bed now. "What? What's wrong, Mama?" I could hear my heartbeat getting louder and louder, as if it was going to jump out of my chest.

My mom sat on the edge of my bed. She picked up my hand. "Early this morning, around one o'clock, two teenagers who had been heavily drinking were killed in a car accident near 75 and Greenville. Those two teens were identified as Cole and Eric."

"No, say it ain't so," I yelled. Tears streamed down my face. "It can't be true. I just saw him last night. Cole doesn't drink, Mom. What you heard can't be true," I repeated over and over.

She rocked me back and forth in her arms.

Danielle wept out loud. "Eric said he had some liquor in the car. I didn't think he was serious. I thought he was kidding."

All eyes focused on her.

"What are you saying, Dani?" I asked, sniffling.

"They're gone, Porsha." She got up from where she was lying and walked over to us.

My mom embraced us both as we tried to deal with the untimely death of two boys who meant the world to us. "Are you going to be okay? I wanted to go reach out to Cole's mom to see if she needed anything."

"We'll be fine," I said. I wiped the tears from my face.

"I can't believe this. I was supposed to call him last night when I got home. With all of the excitement, I forgot. How could I forget?" I yelled.

"We both forgot. Eric wanted to meet up later. I totally ignored his last call."

I rushed out of the bed and retrieved my cell phone from my purse. I saw several missed calls. One was from Cole. I dialed my voice mail and hit the speaker button.

Cole's voice rang from the phone. His words were a little slurred but audible. "Baby, I wish you could be hanging out with us now. We had a few drinks, so I got a little buzz. But I wanted to tell you I love you. I had a great time tonight, and you'll always be my girl."

I heard Eric in the background yelling, "Man, get off the phone. That girl knows you love her. Hang up. We got things to do."

"Bye, baby. Love you," were the last words he said, before the call disconnected.

"He loved me," I repeated over and over, as me and my BFFs rocked each other back and forth.

Less than a week later, I was saying good-bye to a special guy. Turning sixteen was sure to be an unforgettable time for me. Although Cole and I only had a brief time together, I knew he loved me. I loved him too. I would never forget how his eyes sparkled when he saw me. How he laughed at my corny jokes. How I laughed at his corny jokes. The way he went out of his way to make me special. The way he pled with me that last night to forgive him, and I'm glad that I did. The only regret I had was him not hearing me tell him that I loved him too. But a part of me knew he felt the love, or why else would I deal with his silly ways? I chuckled out loud at the few memories we shared. He would forever be in my heart. Though his life was brief, at seventeen he left a lasting impact on a lot of people.

My mom and dad both consoled me as we sat on the second pew at the church where Cole's funeral was being held. Many of our classmates and teachers from school were there to show their respect to the school's fallen basketball hero and to the boy who was my first love. My hand covered his class ring on the necklace he gave me. I would never take it off. It was my reminder of the love we shared.

I listened as Pastor McCormick preached about the dangers of drinking and driving. He was hoping that Cole and Eric didn't lose their lives in vain. He felt like he knew that Cole would want him to share his story. Pastor McCormick said, "One of the young men who survived the crash wanted to say something to the congregation."

Braylon, in a wheelchair and still badly banged up, was helped up to the front and given a microphone. He said, "Our decision to drink and ride around was a poor decision. Please, I beg you, don't drink, and if you do, don't do like we did and get in a car and drive around." In between tears he said, "I came up here today because I don't want anyone to feel the guilt I feel. My two teammates are dead and I'm left behind."

There was not a dry eye in the place after he finished talking. Someone, I assume, his mom, came and wheeled him down the aisle. I watched him as he passed by. I was thinking, *Why couldn't that have been Cole left behind?* I started crying so hard, my mom brought my head on her shoulder as she consoled me.

Walking by Cole's casket on the way out and looking at his cold body laying in the casket was one of the hardest things I'd ever had to do. "Good-bye, my love," I said, as I bent down and kissed his lips for the last time.

My father wrapped his arm around me, and he and my mom escorted me out of the church. We got into our waiting limousine and opted to head straight home.

I remained silent for the rest of the day.

Danielle was also still a little messed up with losing Eric. They weren't as close as Cole and I, but they had made a connection. And Tara tried to ease our pain by listening and crying with us.

One thing I could count on for sure, in times of distress, was my two best friends. We were friends to the end, and they'd proven it to me over and over again.

"I say we have a sleepover and make up our faces like we used to when we were little girls," Tara said.

"I don't know. Maybe another weekend," I said.

"Come on. What about you, Dani?" Tara asked.

"I'm with Porsha. I just want to chill by myself."

"Okay. Well, I'm here if y'all need me."

"Love y'all. I'm going to try to get some sleep," I said, as I hung up and closed my eyes.

Cole was the last thing on my mind as I drifted off to sleep.

EPILOGUE

It had now been two months since Cole's funeral. Getting back into a routine had been difficult. My heart still ached. I doubt if I'd ever get over losing Cole. My grades hadn't improved much, but I was still holding on to my B. My mom didn't pressure me. I was glad she understood. And Dion had become a fixture in my life. I was also happy that he and my first dad were getting along. My mom wasn't too sure she liked their renewed friendship, but I actually did.

The reality show with Jasmine was in full force, now that they'd given me time to grieve. I saw some clips from the show that was set to start airing this summer. Of course they made us out to be rivals. Then again, in actuality, I guess we were. Two rich girls vying for their father's attention was the theme that they wanted to portray. Jasmine still had the upper hand in that area, but she was too blind to see it. I knew that she and Dion had a special bond, like me and Trey had a special bond; neither could be replaced, but there was room in all of our hearts to accept the other. Now, if only Jasmine could see it.

The show's rating should really jump when the producers film me, my BFFs, and Brenda on our trip to the Bahamas. Jasmine still thinks she's going, and even after I told her she wasn't invited, she insisted that she was. If she went, it would be on her own dime. It's not like she didn't have the money for it. We got paid one hundred thousand dollars per show. Official filming of the show would begin as soon as summer started. Instead of harping on the music career that I badly wanted now more than ever, I added a new cause to the show. I asked my mom to help me become a spokesperson for Teens Against Drunk Driving.

Danielle had been dealing with depression, but she was close to being her jovial self. We both agreed to forget boys for a while and concentrate on trying to hold on to our grade point averages. Danielle already had a B, and although she didn't want to admit it, she was glad mine had dropped down to a B too.

She'd better enjoy it, because next year I was going for straight A's again. I was determined not to let anything or anyone stop me this time.

Besides, the drama of this past semester would be hard to top. If I could survive what life dealt me this first half of the year, everything else would be a cakewalk.

I opened up my diary and wrote inside my thoughts of what has happened.

The secrets untold unfolded into a domino effect that had my life spiraling out of control.

A new love brought joy to my life for a brief moment. Sadness filled my life as he departed into another world.

Although saddened by what happened to Cole, joy also filled my life with the realization I had not just one dad, but two dads who cared about me more than anything in this world.

Then I wrote these words on the last page of my journal:

Porsha Marie Swint to the outward eye was nothing but a spoiled little rich girl with a fascination for lip gloss, but she has seen more heartache in her young life than many will experience in theirs. The lessons life taught her will last until the end of her days. Losing Cole left an opening in her heart. Will life will ever be the same? Only time will tell. The end of one stage, and now on to the next.

Website Resources for Teens, and Reasons Why You Shouldn't Drink and Drive

What happened to two of the important characters in *Secrets Untold* was a tragedy. It could have easily been avoided, if they hadn't chosen to drink and drive. This was only fiction. In real life, the impact of making such a terrible decision could be devastating to all involved. Drinking and driving don't only affect the victims, but those they leave behind. Please, as an advocate against drinking and driving, I want to impress upon you to not drink, or get in the car with anyone who has been drinking. It can save your life and someone else's.

Statistics from the CDC (Centers for Disease Control and Prevention):

- According to the CDC, 3,000 teenagers died from fatal car crash injuries in 2009.
- From the same report, more than 350,000 required medical attention from their injuries sustained in a car collision.
- Forty percent of deaths for persons aged 15 to 20 stem from automobile collisions, according to the CDC.

Below are several resources:

Teens Against Drunk Driving:
http://www.teensagainstdrunkdriving.org

- We Don't Serve Teens:
http://www.dontserveteens.gov/dangers.html

- The AAA Guide to Teen Driver Safety:
http://teendriving.aaa.com

- Mothers Against Drunk Driving:
http://www.madd.org/underage-drinking/

- Centers for Disease Control and Prevention: http://www.cdc.gov

AUTHOR'S BIO

Shelia M. Goss is the Dallas Morning News best-selling author of the young adult series, *The Lip Gloss Chronicles*: *The Ultimate Test*, *Splitsville*, and *Paper Thin*. *Secrets Untold* is the fourth book in the series. She's also the *Essence* magazine & Black Expressions Book Club bestselling author of eight books for adults: *My Invisible Husband*, *Roses Are Thorns*, *Paige's Web*, *Double Platinum*, *His Invisible Wife*, *Hollywood Deception*, *Delilah*, and *Savannah's Curse*. Besides writing fiction, she is a freelance writer. She's the recipient of several awards, which include: EDC Creation Award for *The Lip Gloss Chronicles* and honored as a Literary Diva: One of The Top 100 Most Admired African American Women in Literature. To learn more, visit her dedicated young adult website: www.thelipglosschronicles.com or for more information about her other books, visit: www.sheliagoss.com, www.facebook.com/sheliagoss or follow her on twitter at www.twitter.com/sheliamgoss.